The Painted Lady

by
benjamin allen

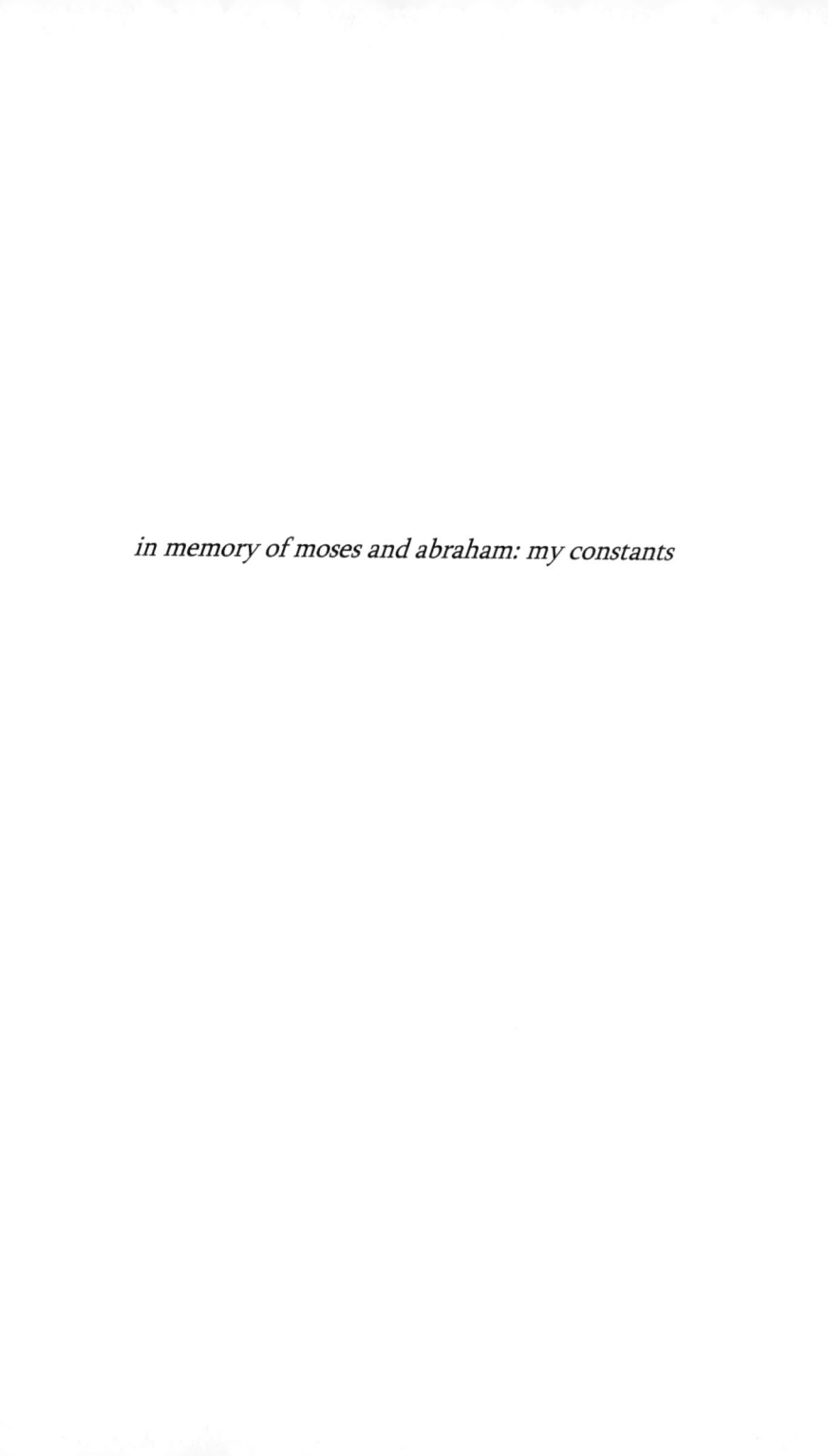

in memory of moses and abraham: my constants

TABLE OF CONTENTS

THE SELFSAME BOLT

"Now I do not know whether I was then a man dreaming I was a butterfly, or whether I am now a butterfly, dreaming I am a man."

   - Zhuangzi

I.

Princess Katreina's disillusionment began when she was fourteen years old, and sneaked from the three-towered fortress of Mirshan castle to the city of Ataraxia, passing the parapet Night Guards with crossbows, who were not accustomed to watching for anyone exiting the premises.

The Emperor, distant and often busy politicking, shielded from her signs of weakness in the human body. The castle halls where she had been permitted he filled with youth and beauty and gardens that couldn't die.

Fourteen years old, and that night she'd witnessed a brutal, vicious, five-minute long street lashing from an armed, uniformed man against a boy who seemed her age. After the guard left, she approached the boy, with a stinging anguish in her heart, and knelt beside him, not realizing the boy – pale, eyes blank, and mouth ajar— was already dead. She asked herself if the cadaver near her arms, then, was to be considered human, and asked herself the same of the officer whose identity she never learned.

An image of the dead might have been traumatizing to her if not for its novelty; she could be twistedly curious, and the image only beckoned her to more often sneak from Mirshan's palace.

Then Katreina's headmistress caught and interrogated her about what she knew of Ataraxia. Katreina cleverly submitted a denial that she'd succeeded on any other occasion and, fearful of being disciplined, gave her sneakiness a rest, continuing her hum-drum studies of flora, stars, maths, and literature, to include a plural secular study of the various religions, all of which bored her to tears.

Again when she was sixteen the itch to escape became an uncontrollable urge, and so she entered the city, this time by day, swearing to herself she could make it home for the nighttime banquet.

Rebellious in nature, she was also calculatedly cautious. She wore a cloak and the dress of a maid, and her first theft was a bouquet of flowers, mint, and basil, which she toted in her hands through the market place; her goal had been to encounter a man. A bread salesman or apprentice smith, someone strong and courageous and a wonder to behold.

The man that caught her eye was nothing of the sort. He was a rapscallion of the lowest order, an impish pinched-up-faced rodent of a man with dreadfully vomit-colored orange hair and was dressed in burlap pants and no shirt, and she hadn't seen him coming, racing as he was down the crowded marketplace, hell-bent upon catching her. He said to himself, "Think you'll get away with that do ya?" repeatedly because he was obsessive. And then, without knowing Katreina was a young woman rather than a man— for the cloak obscured her feminine shape—he socked her at the temple, in plain view of shoppers and sales-folk. She dropped to the dirt and covered her ears, and the flowers and mints and clutches of soil scattered beside her. Her ear drums pounded and she felt dizzy to the degree of extreme nausea, such as the feeling of vertigo. He was barefooted and his feet were scabbed, calloused, and scaly as if strips of skin could peel away like bark from an old oak tree. She glanced upwards once, her eyes glassy from brief pain and fear. He hurriedly collected the flowers, cussing, when he heard,

"She's a girl! Just a girl, how could you?" and the rough teenager, without apologizing, replied, "I dint know and how would I and should it matter since he's a thief? A thief!"

She would get even, and would have to formulate a plan, but her immediate concern was the redness and the bruising on her head quite close to her right eye, and with no way to cover it would conjure a lie from the book of "I was just clumsy" excuses: She stumbled into the corner of the wardrobe.

Only she wasn't known for clumsiness. On the contrary, her miraculous balance was the great jealousy among the dancing troupe; she was often compared to a butterfly, for she kept a comparable flight, with equal if not superior grace, and was the object of affection of all boys her age.

If anybody would have asked— but obvious as the bruise was, no one mentioned it or otherwise showed a care in the world. And therefore she was able to use hats until the swelling faded.

In a fury one night Katreina decided how to get even with him, and her plan involved relentless stalking of his daily patterns, because she intended to rob his house of everything valuable, then quickly give his belongings away for free, to wash her hands of the evidence. She suspected any family situated within the market wasn't suffering for a want in the world, and would therefore possess many riches.

Nothing unfolded the way Katreina originally planned. She was too impatient to stalk her mark and pin down his activities, and the house from whence he emerged was indeed larger than she suspected, his family more numerous. She learned the flower business was for the children, among who the red-headed rodent was one of six, the second oldest. Father's occupation was unknown to Katreina, but, because of the presence of a maid, she figured him for either a laboring foreman or a traveling merchant, but she had no way of knowing.

Soon the desire for revenge overtook her.

At night, while waiting in the market's ring, with only a few merchants and buyers remaining, selling bulk goods like fish, leather, and chests of iron ingots, she witnessed the father of the family enter their gated estate. The house was made of white limestone and resembled a cathedral in its structure but contained neither stained glass, nor idols. No longer tucked in at bed time, she knew there'd be no roundabout questioning from her mistress in the morning, but if she took too long, she'd be reported missing, since it was nearly impossible to sneak in during the day, and difficult enough at night, considering she took advantage of a certain sleeping outpost guard on the North Eastern Wing.

So she circled the house, following the lanterns lit and winking out, in order to locate the father and mother's bedrooms.

Little was she aware of the boy's pension for reading military history texts and playing or recreating battles from wooden and metal soldier miniatures upon his space on the floor. She mistook his room for the master's, since it was the final light to darken.

Ill-conceived plans wonderfully executed begot ill-conceived results.

His room was on the second floor. Her balance from the dance translated well into scaling the wall, albeit slowly, like a slimy snail, because silence was more important than speed. Even on a warm night, the red-headed rodent of a boy shuttered his window, seconds after her climb began, and if she had seen the tan sun-freckled skinny arms, she would have paused, reassessed her plan of entry, or abandoned the venture all together, but she was determined and impatient.

Lemur-like she clung fast to the sill just above her head, which was wide enough to contain empty flower pots and, with one pull up, rest her butt there, giving her time to quietly jig the latch.

Ever-careful not to swipe one of the pots down, her prowess in dancing became useful again. She made not one sound. A few seconds later, she desperately calmed herself. Katreina's heart beat excessively as much from exertion as fear. Well out of view of potential witnesses, she wrestled with a makeshift lock-pick and bent the end to create a kind of L-shaped wrench. No light spilling through the cracks of the shuttered windows, no sounds heard beyond. She stood on the sill after releasing the latch. She inched the shutter open.

But, just on the inside of the room, he waited. The sight of him startled her completely. She fell. He took a handful of her thick dark hair, and she hanged suspended clawing at his arms. His oysterlike body odor and skunkish breath, and the shadow of him: He hoisted her up by her hair, which was ripping, then dragged her into his bedroom. She flung herself against a bedroom wall and before she could scream, he slapped his hand over her mouth.

"So we have this trade in common but I like to keep my goods," the boy whispered. Pressed against the wall, Katreina lifted her knees to her belly and stamped down at his feet, but his control over her was fixed. "Settle down, could you? I'm not actually going to hurt you," but she kicked more violently and thrust him backwards smashing his head against the window frame. "Or, you ungrateful twat, I might snap your neck," he hissed.

Acquiesced, she started to cry.

"Oh no," he said disgustedly. "Don't tell me you're sorry. Don't tell me your daddy beats you."

She cried because he frightened and defeated her, because her boredom with life led her to a choice in which her skills and solitude played against her. Katreina would say none of these things to anyone, especially to a stranger.

Then she relaxed within his arms, secretly re-mapping a way to get him. "So now what?" she said, barely above a whisper. "Turn me over to the guard? Arrest me? Harm me?" and he let her go, knowing she would face him, then.

"Why not train you instead?" His proposition changed his appearance from an ugly vermin into an ivory-carved sculpture.

"You would train me to be a thief, like you? How'd you know I wasn't looking for love?"

The training seemed a lot like partying at night, beneath the open sky and vibrating yellow stars, with Donnely's band of street stalkers. She was the only girl, and the boys were ignorant of her royalty, although in a year, when expected to become the Duchess of a land eastward and take a husband of her choosing, this would be downright impossible to hide.

There wasn't a royal look, for example. Clothes and rolling around in the muck provided enough illusion of a rough life, and so the band of boys felt like they were being charitable, even with unsavory intentions on their minds. The boys were Donnely, Roland, Hopp, Miller, and Wasp, who was the violent one among men of otherwise surreptitious natures. Sure they stole, but not often a lot, and not right away. They targeted the ones who walked home alone and stuck'em up and intimidated with uses of masks and weaponry, especially folks who won at gambling tents or who, at the market, made more than initially predicted, and whose purses were heavy with extra weight in silver.

Katreina enjoyed the excited debauchery of their companionship, but her interest in thievery had nothing to do with obtaining wealth. As a potential job, she proposed to rob a wizard mound of its potions, but was met with nays and naws all around. They didn't believe magic existed, but she said she could prove magic existed.

"Talk about a sniveling little coot," one of them said. "Prove it? How will you prove it?"

"We steal something and test it out. There's stuff like lanterns that burn with no oil, and minotaur costumes that gives you real hoofs," and she shrugged her shoulder.

"Hey maybe if you locate a unicorn we can fly to the moon later," said Hopp. "Holding onto the horn!"

"Entrance to a wizard's tower is difficult anyway," explained red-haired Donnely, wiping his red face of sweat. "But we're thieves, great thieves, likely the greatest known to Mirshan. If you say we're aiming too low, perhaps up the ante. But then we'd need a fence, wouldn't we?"

"Rather a purpose," Katreina corrected. "I've heard of a magical piece of paper that, with the proper magic word shows you faint specks for a coin in the pocket, and thick blocks of ink for denser collections of gold. A wizard in this city is not likely to have them, except, well... except if you're a detective hunting down giant stashes of stolen loot," she explained, sounding very reasonable.

"So we figure out the wizard who's got connects to the coppers," deduced rodent-faced Donnely.

"Lately," said Katreina, "I was thinking you boys were a bunch of blowhards, good for nothings. Time for some real action."

"There are so many risks," said Roland. "Fireballs and stuff."

"But I'm up for a challenge," Donnely said and the boys, quick to please Katreina were on board with her idea.

Before they knew it, the time of the daring robbery was upon them.

Once a wizard of the tower caught them, he turned the whole group of them into the guards, where the guards brutishly interrogated them. Katreina announced she was the Princess of Ataraxia in Mirshan and claimed she was forced: abducted and then forced by all five of them, who took advantage of the outpostman on the quiet wing of the palace.

She admitted she exchanged letters with the criminals, yes. As evidence she procured a few forgeries of these exchanged letters, which were cause enough for the Emperor to sentence Donnely to torture. Soldiers doused the boy in honey, chained him to a canoe, and set him off, afloat the great Myrrh lake, to be eaten alive slowly, by insects. Roland, Hopp, Miller and Wasp were subject to the pillory. At first only Wasp survived the stoning, but having suffered many broken bones and a split skull, he died later as well.

"It was awful, father," cried Princess Katreina, "And it's all my fault!"

"Now now," the Emperor said, fakely consoling her. "Don't you have more important things to worry about? You're supposed to be studying genealogies and birthrights, landowners, the like. Your son is to be Emperor. You're too old for games with ignorant street thugs who can't even break into a wizard's tower. I hope," he said finally and sternly, "You weren't looking for a suitor among those men."

"Among the common folk? No, I'm sorry for them, but no."

"Then run along," said the Emperor. He was wearing a velvet and silk outfit, without the black steel armor, and without the crown. He still seemed somehow above man.

"Oh," she said. "Get rid of that guard, father. He succumbed to bribery."

"Obviously, my daughter and love-light of the world," and then they wished another good night and enjoyed the end of the calamity, without stress or worry upon their hearts or souls, while the florists in the market were minus one child, their second-oldest and strongest.

II.

Love: Find me again, love.

From terrible dreams of the destruction of the Mirshan Empire beneath meteorite fire, Rivyn Quo'rath awoke in hypnagogic fear.

A stinging sensation seared his abdomen.

Beneath him gouts of blood sponged the bed's linens. Snake-like shreds of skin littered his bed. When he inspected the deeply-carved wounds on his ribs, pus and viscous blood dotted his fingertips.

The edges of the wounds were so scabbed they felt upraised like plow tracks in a garden.

Lining his fingernails was the powder of blood.

Beyond the lodging's door, one of the beer maids at the pub where he slept, said, "You have a visitor. Looks to be an officer. He claims you two know each other."

"Not now," whispered Rivyn, kneeling beside his bed, in pain. Then more loudly, he said, "Have him … meet me in a couple of hours," and Rivyn fell upon the stone floor, exhausted and confused.

Early in the evening, swordfish and sausage and brie were to be prepared, and Rivyn, dressed in a color resembling the slate gray of a sea gull's feathers, and a black beret, tasked himself with placing stemless daisies upon each of the tables, when the Night Guard Ameda the Fifth arrived, wearing linen pants, leather shoes with no buckle, thus loose on the feet, and a woolen un-patterned vest that exposed his arms to sun burn.

"Fork it over," said the Night Guard to Rivyn.

Ameda the Fifth, captain of Piraz-dai's Night Guard, worked both sides of the law, and he was generally considered determined, patient, and intelligent—no typical officer.

He knew Rivyn Quo'rath once peddled a drug called 'sol,' a smokable orange painkiller, and intended to use this information to extract more information from him.

Although Rivyn was neither tall nor short and seemed lighter than he really was, the Officer didn't intimidate him.

Rivyn said, "Officer, you need nothing from me I actually possess, so if you could just leave—"

"Yes," said the Night Guard. "In fact I do. A Portrait of the Fey, and if the portrait isn't in your possession, as my sources say, I'm not certain whose, in which case I demand help establishing the motivation for the theft, since we both know the paintings are practically," and this word sounded like slammed-down legal books, "un-sellable."

"How did you hear of the Portraits?"

"Palace talk."

"Ah, Palace talk. Right. Well, I wouldn't say un-sellable, sir," said Rivyn, his lips puckering as if considering a satisfying meal. "Indeed, a potential buyer would require a sharp eye and soft heart—"

"Un-sellable, because too rare, and inimitable, voiding the possibility of forgery."

"Begin believing in ghosts, then, I suspect?"

"Ghosts? Tell me why ghosts mean a damn," answered the Night Guard. "Seriously. I have a couple of moments before I'm due for dinner with my daughter."

"Word on the streets is a ghost controlled the artist, directing him to paint the Portraits, before steering him over a cliff, to his death. Something like that," lied Rivyn.

"I've heard those tales myself," said Ameda. "But they're as worthless as the portraits," whispered the Night Guard as if meant as a stab. "So if you have them, why not fess up?"

"My question is: if they're worthless, why care about them?" asked Rivyn, and resumed placing daisies. "Ah yes," he said, tickled at the sudden insight. "You discover an obscure, suicidal artist's final set of work. You sell the whole lot at an exorbitant price, and become wealthy beyond measure."

"Huge profits are not my interest, you know that."

Six guests arrived, dockworkers in dark dusty tan uniforms.

"That would be too unlawful for you," said Rivyn lowly.

"I need to earn the Emperor's favor for Piraz-dai."

"By cleaning up the city's crime, Ameda?" Rivyn said, and then he laughed. "No, wait—isn't soon the Princess expected to choose her husband? The courier shouts: Princess Katreina will wed Ameda the Fifth, captain of the Night Guard!"

"I admit that has a certain ring to it," said the Night Guard, his eyes becoming hawkish, predatory.

III.

Rivyn Quo'rath knew a thing or two about the Portraits of the Fey, all right.

Months prior, he hired a Rapina man named Aurora to paint the images he continually dreamed, hoping a depiction of her might stop the romantically torturous dreaming. And although painting a spirit or soul was far from Aurora's ambition as an artist, he needed the money, so he agreed.

Within days, in a mad state of ecstasy or trance, Aurora created the Portraits of the Fey. He used coal, waxes, and dyed dust. Upon completion of the portraits, something strange happened: one evening, the young Rapina man, Aurora walked into his home and it appeared turned upside-down, as though robbed—yet oddly none of his belongings were missing.

This incident among others prompted Aurora to correspond with Ataraxia's university specializing in extra-sensory phenomena, where he discussed things like the whispers of children where there were only children miles away, or the slamming of doors when the wind was still.

He even shared with them one of the portraits, but they destroyed it immediately, to avoid any potential disturbances, despite the last letter Aurora received dismissing his claims to experience extra-sensory activity as "self-aggrandizing" and "rabble-rousing."

When Rivyn entered the artist's solitary cottage outside Ataraxia to collect the portraits, he found no trace of the portraits, besides a pile of ashes in the fire place.

This is when Aurora explained to Rivyn about the odd happenings in his home and the consequential correspondence with the university experts of Ataraxia. Upset that Aurora hadn't kept confident about their business, Rivyn purchased the exchanged letters from the university experts and discreetly disposed of them, since for a criminal there is no such thing as good attention; and to make up for his blunder, Aurora gave Rivyn the unfinished portrait he was glad to be rid of anyway, and thus, though not all was lost, Rivyn returned home a little disheartened.

Later, alone at a cheap inn, Rivyn Quo'rath unrolled the canvas, and the beauty of the image immediately enraptured him.

To say this spirit-creature was humanlike would be misleading, for they reminded Rivyn of the astral bodies, except if astral bodies reflected a woman's form. She appeared as he remembered her from the dreams and, as he suspected, for a while the dreams ceased.

Instinctively Rivyn protected the half-finished portrait, but effectively used it once to seduce a woman and, when she described the portrait to another bed fellow—a Night Guard who swore to protect her—Rivyn was given away as the owner of an illicit commodity. After all, a poor lonely bartender wouldn't own expensive things, like rare artwork, unless he'd stolen it.

Fortunately for Rivyn, the woman he slept with remained ignorant of the portrait's power. Sensing he erred in judgment, he made haste to a tomb belonging to a family of displaced foreigners, and planted the portrait within the tomb, to hide it from prying eyes.

A month passed before the Night Guard arrived with a writ of investigation into Rivyn's personal quarters, Ameda claiming to search for the drug, but the search turned up merely one item of contraband: a pipe with the residue of banned incense.

It was enough to punish Rivyn, however, and Ameda forced him to labor at his estate, which was well-known to the public, and there, during work in the corn fields—husking, cleaning, and blading the corn—Rivyn asked to see the writ of investigation and Ameda explained he was also under scrutiny over a stolen painting, and Rivyn, because of his keen intuition concerning devious minds, cheerfully made Ameda an offer. "If hypothetically, you sold intoxicants on the side, I could be of great assistance to you, by naming your competition, though not from personal experience."

"Your price would be, hypothetically?"

"Lots of freedom to operate," answered Rivyn, after gestured to rake a dry patch of failing corn stalks.

"Problem is," said Ameda, "I don't know your trade."

"My trade? It's very simple," said Rivyn. "I'm a bartender who cleans mugs. And when I'm released from your temporary indentured servitude, never come bother me again."

"Or what? One night I'll find my daughter's vertebrae shattered from an upstairs fall? Every time a thug threatened me he didn't live to regret it."

Rivyn said, "The choice is yours. No such 'threat' exists if we lack another truly unwarranted interrogation.

I'm sorry your concubines are fiction-feeders and like to ruffle your feathers."

A week later, outside of Rivyn's place of occupation, Ameda approached him with a counter-offer of pearl tears for a layout of the south end's drug trade.

Rivyn agreed he could betray the top dogs if Ameda allowed the peddlers who exercised the leg work to continue without interruption.

"Do you have a fondness for street urchins?" asked Ameda.

"Only because I was one," Rivyn nodded absently, but added, "A long time ago."

"None then shall lose the food brought their lips. I'm no tyrant," said the Night Guard.

After leading Ameda to his upstairs lodging, Rivyn popped a bulbous cork off a peach, pear, and apple wine. "This shall seal the deal, captain. Share some of this wine with me, will you officer? If you've drunk anything like it, and can name its exact source, I'll give you the information you seek for free. If not, you'll owe me extra."

"I will agree on the condition you provide proof of my ignorance," said the Night Guard, holding out his cup.

"One hint: it is a very rare wine," said Rivyn.

Evening was setting upon the lodge, and a meadow of fog curled into the wide gray brick muddy streets and brought with it a cold humidity.

Rivyn's room was like the hut of a hermit, with a cot covered with wool and hay, and a night stand with plate and cup, yet there was no seat and minimal decoration besides an open trunk inlaid with a gilded tree engraved upon its surfaces. To Ameda it stored flimsy old blankets and one of Rivyn's cloaks; there was nothing special or peculiar about it.

In reality, the trunk was a magical wormhole—anything dropped into it would appear within one of its duplicates (there were no more than four)—but the thief cleverly used a false-bottom to evade suspicion and keep his belongings from floating in limbo.

Rivyn's hand covered his mug. He was eager for the Night Guard, who sat upon the floor, to take the first swig of the wine, but eventually the two sipped at the same time.

The tastes and textures enthralled Ameda, who belted out a hearty laughter, the kind that seemed possible only by a fire in the middle of the night. "Delightful!" he cried, and gripped the mug now with both hands. "You're certain this is no elixir, not drugged or spiced with magic dust?"

"Many of the ingredients are unknown to me personally," answered Rivyn coolly.

"Empty," said the Night Guard and held forward his mug as if knocking a dead tree from his path in the woods. "Refill my cup so I may become more educated."

"Give it up! You don't have a hair's breadth of a clue where it's from, and if you're not busy, the drink is better conserved. I'll part with one tongue's worth, and that is all. But careful, Ameda, that it doesn't cloud your judgment."

"Oh it's not potent enough to," and he hiccupped, and his cheeks scolded redly. "A taste," he said, then Rivyn splashed some into his mug, which entered the Night Guard's mouth in one motion. He washed the wine around and sucked the back of his teeth. He gargled and swallowed the wine and suddenly seemed uptight.

"Don't know?" asked Rivyn Quo'rath. "You don't know."

"All right you caught me. I can't place it. The fruits are out of season, so I guess it is a wine of twenty-two years, five months, and four days, with hours adding upon it now. You made it, didn't you?"

"With royalty in your blood and everything. For shame you can't identify this wine. You owe me extra, now, but I'll tell you you're correct about everything you've said, except for the age," said Rivyn.

"I believe I taste lilies."

"That little detail is irrelevant, now. So if you must know I appropriated the bottle from your ill father's quarantine bedroom, but how had I known of his drinking and you didn't? Before you object or attempt to argue with me, here, take it to him. Be by his side while he awakes."

"No," said the Night Guard Ameda with a look of dismay and honest surprise glossing over his countenance. "It would be impossible. Too many guards on staff," but he held the cork and wine within one hand.

"They are greedy, lazy, unobservant little gamblers, your guards. There was no bloodshed, thank the goddesses. I know your family sleeps there, too."

Suddenly Rivyn excused Captain Ameda the Fifth from his private lodging, and while Ameda felt frustrated, baffled and outright enraged, he showed no emotion, for though Rivyn violated his estate, his objective was to hint at his true occupation. Thus the Night Guard Ameda began scheming. How might he manipulate this petty sneak-thief towards the fulfillment of his own ends?

IV.

A month after Katreina's incident, the Emperor attempted to cancel a certain feast, but Empress Felicity talked him into allowing the scheduled activities, for, she explained, they expected literally hundreds of folks from at least three cities each to be in attendance and, she added, politics is defined by the people we move "hither and thither."

All the greater reason to cancel the event, then, he stated.

Certainly, she replied straight-forwardly, if you want to be viewed as one gigantic ass.

And that night he railed her in bed and reclaimed his dominance, but the intended feast, as she wished, was still on its way.

Empress Felicity enjoyed the colors, smells of exotic foods, and shows of artistic merit, the dancing troupes, residential painters, sculptors, and poets. So rare is a talented and disciplined poet who scribes and performs aloud with equal delight, she thought. The Emperor would be able to keep his mouth full, and shut, chewing on meat spiced to his taste; his opinion would be unnecessary. Furthermore he'd have no hand in any of the planning or execution, simply the pleasure, and in turn this pleased Empress Felicity.

By the way she was well prepared to handle gossip on her daughter's behalf. An interested suitor might step forward to make an impression upon Katreina – in fact there'd be many such individuals, and the Empress would feel obligated to bite her tongue, reserve judgment of these men till later, and resign herself to an observing role.

All quite painfully relieving, like that of pulling a rotted tooth.

Among the other activities was a game of rrokcha bones between two genius mathematicians who were champions of their vassals—and this game was intended to be surrounded by a flood of lesser games involving, by contrast, insignificant stakes, for this game placed into the pot a total of four rich farms that neighbored each other. All this started because the peasants working so-and-so's farms began complaining to the peasants of such-and-such's farms, about taxes, which catapulted the two landholding vassals into a verbal bickering. They decided to settle their quarrels like gentlemen, before the royal family.

Empress Felicity was interested in the victor, for both knights held great wealth, and unlike other knights, ruled with austerity and applied complicated channels of bureaucracy, so during any given day they wouldn't be bothered to judge the affairs of common scum.

There she thought specifically of the knight Ameda, who, despite his status, worked the streets as a guard. A captain, yes, well-respected and earning tributes so extraordinarily fair none could despise him. He would be in attendance.

So it was. In fact Ameda and a small group of cohorts were the first to arrive that morning, well before Katreina tightened her corset and unwound her stockings and snaked her head through a pearl necklace, applying a miraculously deep brown eye shadow that, beneath, was streaked with the pink of a soft evening's sunset, before the dress of silk and cotton fell to her ankles. She appeared sexy and somber, as if both mourning and triumphant.

By a royal standard Ameda, looking his best, was still ugly. Time and stress took its toll. If he'd let go of the executioner's rope and ax, wind would not cut so deeply into his wrinkles. He should marry soon. He was without family, except a father, aunts and uncles, and brothers who didn't make it past their late teens.

Felicity observed him from a distance, too sneakily for Ameda to notice. She'd been ready just after dawn, spending this time arousing her grump of an Emperor and husband, who flailed awake late from nightmares involved by that mad combination of wine, liquor, and drug. "It's prophetic, taps right into god's great plan," he said.

Ameda's cohorts were all men, armed until their uniform broad blades were racked beside their black skull hats.

They were invited to sit for chocolate and walnut cakes made with molasses from across the Myrrh Lake, and to wait patiently for the other guests. The table, marble-topped but otherwise mahogany could accommodate forty men, and this was one table of three in the great hall. Ten others like Ameda were to be scrunched together and essentially forgotten about, although nothing disallowed them from asking for guidance to another station. Of course this was their game, to command notice.

Mirshan Castle's main hall, where these gentlemen pecked at their morning appetizer was where most visitors were permitted, since it was in line with a direct path to the gate. The main hall, however, did not really lead anywhere forty men, all collectively thinking the same thing could penetrate, and therefore compromise royal blood. In fact an architect with the print in hand would be able to demonstrate the main hall's basic disconnection from the rest of the castle, including all three towers.

One path led to the gardens and stone tablet library, filled with fountains, fruit trees (especially plum trees, for plums most pleased the Emperor), grape and honey suckle vines, and five pyramid-shaped stone huts with telescopes tilted skyward. Inside these huts were dates and corresponding coordinates and the etched titles of constellations.

These areas were heavily guarded and under the watch of the Dark Horse Company, rather than the knights whose hands had never felt the grime and tar and oil from truly handling weaponry.

Here the Emperor would indifferently look down upon the game of rrok-cha, and become throne-drunk, which meant only intoxicated from loss of breath, bested by even the shortest of speeches, and too much attention upon himself. After a sniff of juniper ale he might just fall asleep like a full-bellied child. This was also the station reserved for incoming artists, competing for royal funding, hired by knights, who, in their desire to inscribe themselves upon history, used self-portraits to supplement their legacies, and paid dearly for the artist with flattering visions of their flaws.

Three hundred seats: a small feast and more important to the guests than the hosts, something indeed the Emperor understood and why, when glancing at his calendar that morning, wouldn't mind allowing it to pass, suitors be damned. He didn't comprehend why they, mother and father, rulers of the Mirshan Empire, could not simply choose the wealthiest duke with the greatest accomplishments, and wish their daughter Katreina a joyful life of leisure. No, there needed to be a faint illusion of free will on her part.

It would have been Ameda's third cocoa when the feast really began; he pouted because he couldn't manage to speak with the Empress, what with her snooty display of absence and the herding of this 'worker echelon' out of view, but when other guests were directed to the outside festivities, he made a show of patience, and led his cohorts into the long line, leaving behind the empty dishes that were perhaps not intended to be filled in the first place.

Something the guards would consider sinister happened at this time.

An artist, named Aurora, whose primary work would be propped up before the knights with no taste except for their vanity, had somehow slipped into Katreina's costume closet, which, while still blocked off from the vital halls was strictly off-limits to any man, and especially one of his status.

What was he doing?

Putting the make on Princess Katreina with honeyed words and un-dramatic, bluntly-stated desires. He slipped her a gift, and when giving in to his advances, she curtsied, exposing her thighs and a little glimpse of her little buttocks. She hid the rolled-up canvas behind a fox-fur cape so long it spilled onto the floor. And she shoo'd him away, knowing if caught he'd become the victim of royal torture. He whispered his name to her and she gave him her neck to be kissed, but he did not dare disgrace her, and even this chivalrous act made her giggle, she merely imagining his moist lips and stubbly mustache hairs upon her skin. He stomped his foot playfully like a dumb animal and inhaled modestly her scent of wisteria and vodka, and then somehow the quick-footed, darkskinned vagabond made it back to the festival ground without being spotted or rousing suspicion.

Katreina fell in love with Aurora then and immediately. It was he who helped attain her vengeance, after all, providing the forgeries of a man's script, and even more so, she fell in love with the allowance to take on extra-marital affairs, resigned to be sold, to whoever, for the worth of four farms, its peasants, goats, sheep, chickens, and long-haired buffalo. She was soil equally fertile for the birth of children, and romance was the stuff of giddy young girls.

But, a path became clear for an affair to thrive between Aurora and Katreina, involving Felicity's secret approval, given Katreina neither become too attached to this man of rather poorly defined origins, however lovely he might seem, nor make promises to him she could not keep.

V.

Violet swarms of thunder clouds. Clouds spiraled beyond the peninsula coast of Ri'shurai. Each crashing wave left traces of this skyborn ambrosia imprinted upon quartsand mud. A pattern was half-discernible through the arched window of a lake-side lounge called the Dream Collective, where Cohis Brayhem smoked, contemplating gossip he overheard from dining officers, who were concerned with the death of a woman he loved.

It was longer than ten years ago. Eriella was a sturdy, stoic, hard-souled woman, lethally attractive, and new to the city. She migrated there because she suffered the deaths of a husband and two daughters to northern plague, and yet with her remaining son, she managed a life of peaceful waging. He was poor and without skill, his future close-at-hand and indeterminate. They reached for the same mango at Spouter Bay's low market. A mango she intended to purchase, and he to steal. She invited him to enjoy dinner and he was too emaciated to decline. Some would say they fell in love.

She fed and nurtured him. He protected her son and taught him how to play games and fish the shallow of the great lake. Her sex was joyful, energetic, and revived in him the innocent memories of his youth, like when his mother massaged his temples to soothe an earache, or when she sang from the threshold of their cottage to the ding of fork and pan, reviving in him the same excitement he felt at dropping everything he'd been doing (remembering none of that now), taking off as with winged feet bounding home, squeezing past her at the door in a bee-line toward the table overfull with steaming bowls of brown rice, tender fish, and bulbous red berries gathered off forest shrubs. From these he sucked the jaw-clenchingly sour juices and saved at least one of them for his mother.

In actuality, Cohis used Eriella for survival, he remembered. Her son Samson was still quite young and curious, with slight mean streaks, and she was no soldier, no ready or willing combatant in a city where cutting throats was essentially permissible. She said Cohis' eyes were brighter than a Coyote's, and magically cruel, as if he could view earth and history from two distinct souls, and that anyone in their right minds would fear him.

The coals of his tobacco pipe smoldered and gave the aroma of papaya and cinnamon. The sun was setting. As Cohis watched the animal-hide wearing darkskinned portsmen with damaged dented bones, their hands like gloved cleavers hitching wet-dark crates and nets wet-heavy and dripping gray water from wild-hair seaweed and wriggling lobsters and crabs, lugging them from ships to empty carts awaiting on land, he recalled when he and Samson threw minnow-baited hooks from the piers and cast nets beneath them, bringing back several small edible fish, but one that was quite bloated, and strangely limp.

That night, when Cohis asked to help gut and clean their haul, Eriella became defensive— "It's done – we're done," she said, guarding over the raw meat as if behind her were her daughters, patients sick in their death cots. But Cohis had seen over her broad shoulder the slit of glinting blue light, her face flash a kind of momentary paralysis, and then she said, "Please don't."

"Don't what?" he said dumbly, his voice choked out from a wounded anger.

"Don't ruin this for Samson and me."

"Listen – I don't know where that came from," he said, pointing at a gleaming gemstone nested within a slop of fish guts.

She snapped. "Stop it! Shut your mouth now. I will not live with a filthy crook."

"You're accusing me of theft?"

"Quiet yourself. Yelling around my boy."

"I didn't even – I swear," he whispered, desperately pleading his case. "Why would I ruin the only goodness I know?"

She didn't believe him. To her there was no love between them, only necessity. She ordered her confused child to play in the sand of the alleyway, while Cohis wrapped up his few belongings. He couldn't resist her; his love of her was too strong to ignore even a most painful command.

For days, he rested against a pillar down by the ports watching the ship's shadows come and go. He felt betrayed, helpless, frustrated. And by the time his courage welled within him and he walked to her home with his hat in one hand and a bundle of coal-smudged poems in the other, Eriella and Samson had vanished. The small cottage was empty and abandoned and quiet.

VI.

In Ri'shurai, Rivyn Quo'rath asked around for this man, who was called Cohis Brayhem by his mother, and Coyote by his associates and who'd become, over the past decade, a capo of the city's criminal guild.

For Brayhem, Rivyn had in mind a lucrative proposition for which most of the difficult work was already finished, except for the abduction of Princess Katreina, the crux of his offer.

All sane men knew the price of a woman's safe return contained no nameable number, unless that woman was some kind of royalty, and the months that lay ahead of Katreina determined her entire future.

Now Rivyn needed to arrange a return for his work. The preparations were installed.

He would help Aurora continue his affair with Katreina, removing her from the strict security of the palace. His magical wormhole chests were separated by hundreds of miles, to facilitate the payment.

A pink Solus descended upon the northwestern ports. Great dog-eared masts of transportation ships became silhouettes and towering shadows. Broken here or there by lanterns lighting on the main veins leading north to the heart of Ri'shurai.

A confidante was supposed to meet him outside a closed watchmaker's hovel at sun down; Rivyn was early, but it wasn't until he lit a smoke and blew two rings in a row that an intermediary to the Coyote showed his face. He was fourteen or so years old, and skeletal, and dirty.

"This way," said the boy, and his voice was shy though neither fearful, nor meek. He wore a heavy cotton cloak and his boots were full of holes, such a thin leather they were, and clearly too big, meant to be worn for a couple more years. Abruptly he spun around, and said, "he's on the beach pier." He pointed, with a crooked – perhaps broken and not properly mended finger – down a few blocks, through a stone archway meant for citizens rather than dockworkers or the Night Guard.

"Open your hand," said Rivyn and the boy accepted a tip. "Now tell me," he continued, "How many are watching us or listening?"

The boy grinned and didn't answer. "He wants your business, not the silvers you'd throw to the homeless."

"Fair enough," answered Rivyn, his question's purpose not considered. How high up had Brayhem advanced since the days of cutting purses and stalking gamblers?

There he was though, all by his lonesome, hair tied up, hugging his own knees and gazing upon the oily gray lake, seated several feet from the furthest reaches of the tide.

"Ah! You know we could have met over an autumn ale," said Rivyn.

"It's quiet here," said Cohis, glancing backwards. "Sometimes I prefer the quiet."

Rivyn sat in the sand beside another criminal closest to his own abilities but coming from a completely different background, city, and way of thieving.

Brayhem smiled. His teeth were yellow and crooked, but made that way, as if with plated gold. His smile didn't express joy, but a tinge of lunacy or woundedness, as if challenged. "If we are competitors."

"Which we are not."

"If you live in Ri'shurai, you are my competitor. So what you've brought today must be big. I know you by reputation, so don't be offended if I skip the cum-shot contest and not forget we work the same side of the law."

"What do you know about the artist of the Portraits of the Fey?"

Brayhem's smile grew wider, as if he possessed fangs to bear. "I heard he vanished. A robber destroyed his paintings, even the work having naught to do with Her. Why do you ask?"

Rivyn said, "Is that all you know?"

"That's what I've heard – And rumors about his secret courtship with Princess Katreina. Like he could shut up about something as serious as that. Hah! Could you?"

"No."

"A finer piece of ass hasn't graced Mirshan since ..."

"Haven't seen it."

"Her. You haven't seen her."

"Her ass. You said a 'fine piece of ass.'"

"So I did."

"How much do you think it's worth to the Emperor?"

"Ahh," said Brayhem high-pitchedly, almost like an extended sigh. "A dead canary," he said and licked his lips. "Any price nameable."

"Throw one out there."

"I can't do it."

"Whatever it is, we take ten percent of it each. That leaves you and yours quite a stretch richer. I'm thinking at least two years of an income earned over a ten-day. Who's keeping track of your money?"

"The guild has bookkeepers." Brayhem eyed Rivyn suspiciously.

"First of all, you needn't think I'm trying to sting you. Your people could bail you out and now you're more valuable to them than ever. It's all prepared, set up, but I needed an interested party, could only think of one."

"How soon?"

Striking a second cigarette, Rivyn said, "Within three months, maybe two."

"Have mercy on us, could you? What is your angle?"

"I abduct her. Your people collect the ransom and return her back alive."

"But it's not exactly a ransom is it?"

"Not exactly an abduction, either. No."

Cohis shook his head slowly. "How will you convince Aurora to shut up?"

"That's easy. Sneak him inside the palace." Rivyn stood up, brushed sand off his clothing, a look of disgusted dismay on his face, and said, "In reference to your boss's concerns: Ask him what this is from," and dropped the golden tree inlay from his magical wormhole chest onto the sand at Brayhem's feet. "And what they might be good for."

Days later they met up again, at a pub. A beer maid wearing a hip-length linen skirt and no top served Brayhem and Rivyn tea cups of moonshine, which tasted like bouquets of lilacs, lemon, and lantern oil. They sat by the fire pit, and it gave off minimal heat. Other patrons, by and large, a raucous bunch, full of boyish jest and carnivorous expression, were in greater groups.

"I fucked the shit out of her asshole," said Brayhem coyly, smirking, gesturing toward one of the dancers. "And she licked it off my cock afterwards."

"You must have paid for that."

He shrugged his shoulders. "Listen. Right down to it. Boss doesn't want you anywhere near us during the payment process unless you join our ranks. I said flatly you wouldn't want to. The boss relented on this point, but he smells a problem. Too good to be true, that sort."

Rivyn swigged the moonshine and its deliciousness distracted him.

"I will need your real angle, but I think I understand it now. You know what happens to thieves who are thick with pigs?"

"Oh bite your nasty-ass tongue," said Rivyn. He adjusted his black beret. He lined his lips with the moonshine and sniffed, cleared his throat. "It's like this. A simple officer's goal is to enforce the law, to make arrests when criminals transgress laws. A crooked cop's goal is to obtain wealth and power by any means necessary. I'll submit neither wealth nor power to any who would use them against me, whether to control my movements or send me back to prison."

Brayhem curled his index and middle fingers, seductively and also sleazily, beckoning their topless hostess to the table. "You'll have another," he insisted. When the woman returned, Brayed dropped a stack of coins onto the table, so she'd reach for them, and their hands met upon the stack, he said, "Dance for me, will you?"

Her body was supple, healthy, and her limbs elongated and tubular, her nipples seemingly swollen with milk. Brayhem slipped his hand under her skirt. She pretended not to notice, and instead slid her hair from her eyes. Black hair, shiny like volcanic glass. "He can watch. I got your money baby," he said and then slowly at first with no music rhyming with her motions she swayed her hourglass hips in the shape of infinity. He continued their business, saying: "I'll need an exact date," and then he paused to swallow. "For the delivery that is," and he said it this way to make it seem like he was talking about drugs, which was typical business in Ri'shurai. "Boss wants your chests."

"Not possible."

"For moving the money."

"What's his offer? And it better be good."

"Not for keeps, calm down," said Brayhem, while the lovely dancer began grinding her privates against his, moaning into his ear. "Boss don't trust magic shit, so he's offering something else, and lots of it. As a sign of business honesty – do that again," he said to the woman, and the she dragged her booty down toward Brayhem's knees. "That pussy is tighter than a child's mouth," he said, and Rivyn knew he shouldn't laugh, but did anyway.

"They're invaluable," said Rivyn.

"You get them back with your second installment."

"Do I seem naive to you?"

"We both know why you're using the cop. He's probably as crooked as he could possibly be – and just getting his feet wet, too. Maybe this is all his idea. Anyway I look at it, he's your leverage against me, so consider the offer good, because my guild don't have a standing army. We trick you off your shit and you make disaster for every motherfuckin criminal in Ri'shurai."

"So let's see what you got."

The dancer's plush lips embraced Brayhem's mouth. She closed her eyes. Her expression was of ecstasy. He removed a small pouch from a belt loop. Rivyn opened the pouch.

Seeds. Sol. Citrine. The drug.

"A mere portion," whispered Cohis.

Afterwards Rivyn rolled a smoke and stood smoking against a building, watching workers hit the night shift. In Ri'shurai, almost all of the dockworkers and warehouse loaders received a 100 percent bonus from the treasure trove of the guild, in exchange for ignorantly smuggling—but there was an unspoken, unwritten agreement that if any one dockworker became too nosy, he'd die in a fatal boating accident.

Rivyn decided it was best now he spied on Brayhem's apprentice Makaila, because the boy's occupation for the guild was collecting corner money from drug sales and directing the cash to more mathematically-competent hands.

A few days of observation gleaned Rivyn the information Makaila met Isabel, a girl his age, through selling the drug. The two became something of partners in crime; she helped Makaila with his job and could obtain higher prices, using these profits to support her own use. Rivyn followed Isabel home, and found she was one of three triplets, and the only offspring of a dockworker and housekeeper who were still relatively young, as though, at this rate, Makaila and Isabel would follow their footsteps into parenthood.

What interested Rivyn here was Isabel's semi-resemblance to Princess Katreina. Their hair and skin colors differed, slightly: Katreina's hair was deep and dark, and Isabel's a sun-bleached dandelion blond. Katreina's rich golden skin radiated where she walked, Isabel's sun-baked gritty skin only seemed dark because dirty.

Up close, as Rivyn made his passes, allowed the observation that Katreina, born into this world may well have been the quadruplet of the family.

The two young girls also had something peculiar in common: the ability to formally dance. And both were beautiful too, he thought, and could only become more so with maturity. This girl's breasts were still unfilled-out, and her hips had yet to widen, the weight of her thighs seemed created too soon to burn away or become regular fat. She was the only one who used, and it was obvious with a glance she'd made it too much of a habit – watery dilated eyes, chapped lips, sunken cheeks, like the crinkled shadows of a mountain side.

He let this sad young girl from his thoughts then, for his real intent was to obtain enough information about Ri'shurai's drug trade to fool Ameda.

Now Brayhem's boss, the de facto kingpin, and his wife gave the world four sons, two of who were jewelers. He would say it was one of them who secretly supplied the northern cities with its Sol, using the armed caravans moving jewelry as a nigh untouchable cover operation.

Accounting for the travel time, he figured his little white lie would require an otherwise unfounded search into their caravans to disprove; better then, these shipments were rare and rather secretive themselves.

Rivyn Quo'rath found a place to sit outside the foray of late evening business, and sighed. He couldn't think clearly; the bustle of business was so loud, he couldn't any longer feel distinct from his environment.

Unlike other cities Rivyn frequented he enjoyed how Ri'shurai seemed to have built itself around the cypresses and pines and the strange palm-like trees along the shore, instead of reserving them for parks, cemeteries, or the country-sides. It gave the city a flowing, amorphous shape, in several cliff-like steppes.

The wind grazed over his face and stole his beret, but he was quick enough to catch it with his hand, grinning then to no one, against the street sounds, beneath the falling sun light.

VII.

Headmistress Cerys rushed Princess Katreina from bed two hours before the opening of the eye of Solus through her heavily draped and shuttered tower window.

"Water's heated and the soaps in their cups," she said, and her scowling visage, the first thing Katreina rested her fuzzy gaze upon, repulsed her.

"I swear to the serpent I'll kill you, Cerys. I'll order your year-long torture. Don't think I'm capable? Your hair will string an infant's lute, and what's worse, the follicles will still be attached!" and she flung to her belly and clutched her pillow, her hair, the ivory-white sheets.

"Be that as it may," said Cerys with sardonic sympathy. "Yet your guards are nowhere to be found," then she jerked Katreina by the neck of her gown, but Katreina leaped to stand, whirling around, assuming herself an uncivilized animal, except wearing violet linens.

More calmly, Cerys said, "the bath is to moisten your muscles, Katreina. No man shall take in your scent except when you dance."

"I won't dance," she said, becoming the girl before the woman. "The suitors are – all of them – buffoons. I'd sooner unhinge my cunt to a mastadon's sharpest tusks than endure a lame-cod eunuch whose virility stems from the boiling blood of his peasantry."

She hopped off the bed, her hair ratty and seemingly thick with thorns. "But the water's hot, but you'll massage my thighs, but you'll dress me, but you'll straighten my hair, but you'll…and you'll." She stuck her finger in her mouth, as though forcing herself to gag.

Cerys followed closely behind Katreina. "Just think," she said, "of the hissy pissy fits your husband will be forced to contend with."

"Ugh! And for the wealth he is gaining the advantage, is he not?" she said, not looking back as they hit the corridors to the bath quarters, coated with a gauze of lilac-scented steam. She shook her gown off overhead, and trampled upon the gown advancing to the small circular tub, where beside it was a cauldron and wide ope window.

"Not at all. He will have no rights to your wealth—but if a son is born of your body," corrected Cerys.

"Mmm," hummed Katreina, sinking her left foot into the steaming water. "And now for the second foot," she sang to herself, gently easing herself onto the finely sanded wooden bench. "Oooo," she sang. "Now the oatmeal Cerys, and the eucalyptus, you best hurry too. Mmmmm."

When Cerys returned, Katreina's feet were propped up in front of a rather ugly utilitarian stool, and she said, "If this were all there was to life, you and I taking turns working out the knots from each other's feet, I should die contentedly, and with the wisdom of the willfully ignorant and apathetic."

"Your fingers are too weak to probe the tenderness behind these calluses and dirt, Princess. T'is why I've married a military man, on the by and by. A man who once built a barricade for his squad overnight, out of wood and brick. Maybe keep such details in mind on the opposite end of this very important day."

"Should I reject each of them?" asked Katreina, with a sincerity and vulnerability Cerys considered crushing.

"Legally," said the headmistress, lathering oil upon Katreina's ovaline toes. "You could take a magpie for your lord, Katreina. Or no husband at all."

"The pressure is in favor of marriage and wealth and plump fuckin children, Cerys."

"Don't cuss at me, little missy. You only have little value for wealth because you're literally submerged in it—do you think farmhands have the luxury of silken beds? Everyday baths? Oiled foot rubs? No, their homes are vermin-infested. They lie down with field mice, ticks, fleas, spiders the size of behemoths, and snakes that could pulverize you with one swallow."

"And how should I know these intimate details imprisoned here, with my next seventy years planned?"

Cerys seemed hurt. Trying with all her spiritual might to empathize with the Princess, she still couldn't fathom her tremendous burden. She wouldn't, trapped here, with so few decent suitors, find romance—and to make life in the city below was out of the question. "Focus your depression and anxiety down to your heels, Princess, so I may rub em out like I might squash a spider."

There were five candles lit upon a shelf to Katreina's left, and from her periphery could make out a flame jostling against quick inhales of wind. She silenced a panic, realizing she had been avoiding the encroaching, despairing future, belonging to which she, in a moment of clairvoyant lucidity, could not imagine herself both happy and old.

At dusk Ameda entered his afflicted father's infirmary with the bottle of wine in which remaining was backwash, since Ameda finished it in his lonesome, to the effect of an incredible stupor. His father, also named Ameda, the

Fourth, hated his first-born son for his devotion to the streets and inability to find marriage before any of his younger siblings who took residence within Ameda the Fifth's estate. He hated him further for self-righteousness and fake humility and lack of idols, having little reverence for either gods, or traditions of order.

"Leave me a dignified death," he said to his son, "Your shadow upon me is disgraceful to the point of," and he weakened, his voice straining unto a weak wheezing. "Well – you humiliate me."

"I thought you'd be happy to see me. I've returned with your drink. If it were grain ale I'd excuse it for a cough medicine, but this... this is to kill your liver, I believe." Ameda sat on the edge of his father's bed and sighed. "I stand before Princess Katreina on the morrow. I believe our family, estate, and the work you so despise creates an attractive proposal."

"I'd offer my advice but like a fool you'd simply pretend I hadn't ·spoken. Don't be there. Don't go. Stop thinking about it. You're a disgrace to this entire family. You're the epitome of a man's failure." He coughed and curled into himself, grabbed his stomach and clutched his mouth, shedding soft tears born of anguish. "Why bother me?"

Ameda inched toward his father's head and took the gray swath of hair in his hands, and the paleness of his skull was like a phantom of light. He sighed and huffed and sawed his teeth together. Ameda the Fifth stroked his father's sweaty hair.

"I won't again bother you, father," said Ameda the Fifth, and then fluffed the feathers in his pillow and lay his shoulders at the pillow's base. And then the night guard

Ameda slid out from beside his father, crept to the door, crossed its threshold, exited, and latched the door, leaving the old man cringing and clawing at naught except darkness.

That night Ameda the Fifth dreamed of a starlit woman whispering into his ear, to rouse him from a comatose slumber. Against gravity, they soared through the ceiling as if each were ethereal non-matter levitating up, while below them clouds descended and his back was to the densely empty sky, while the city and surrounding pastures became infinitesimally small.

He called her name, because he knew it was she who imprinted herself upon his imagination— this princess. And greater distances they soared, puncturing the atmosphere of Aerth, floating among burning lights that seemed so close they could be embraced, so distant as to provide no warmth. "I fear you," he whispered, sleepily. And then, in the company of Gods and Goddesses, they descended, harshly, madly, spiraling, and Ameda closed his eyes to avoid the impact of the fall – before he awoke, a sound like an automaton's heart beat against his ears.

When he awoke, his hand instinctively reached for a half-empty bottle of whiskey, a cure for a cog-grinding headache: One full mouth and swallow and exasperated groan. This used to be a rare occasion.

Dreaming of her should have seemed like a blessing. Yet he felt discouraged, because his family badgered him not to make a second appearance in her court. Why couldn't he realize that, to Princess Katreina, he was an insignificant thing? And instead, for some reason unbeknownst to anyone else, he felt worthy of her.

The Princess may well have sought a complement to herself, also someone like-minded. Yes, he judged himself ugly compared to her, and he thought this especially that morning trying to smooth bags from under his eyes and powder out the cavernous dark circles, to brush his hair this way or that way, attempting to cover patches of thinness and failing. His smile used to be charming, although not that charming, and time broke him down in every aspect. Perhaps, he thought to himself, she is not shallow or I am attractive to her. I'm a rarity, a delicacy of a man, an acquired taste.

He was depressed, feeling conflicted, too proud of his accomplishments to rule himself out of the eyes of the Princess, yet feeling these accomplishments meant as much to her as to the city he served.

His hands were gnarled and dirty, encrusted with permanent grease no amount of lye could expunge. He wore silver gauntlets reminiscent of chain-mail armor, with white linen tunic, black scarf round his neck, its frayed ends silver. He wore black cotton breeches, tied with a black leather belt, the buckle pure silver and shaped like a wide-set diamond; and lastly he wore black leather moccasins, and spent an hour polishing them so they shined into his silver chain-mail leggings, a soft expensive cotton pantaloon pressing through. He shaved his neck and allowed the beard, for it was full enough to appear neatened, so he carefully neatened his beard.

None of this satisfied Ameda; he felt ugly and inadequate and there was no more to think upon the subject.

As he was planning to depart, his cousin Clemency, breast-feeding her infant, passed him in the cooking quarters, near the backside stairwell exit, and said, "You look terrible, stay home, you're needed here Ameda. You look so terrible," but he just nodded, fleeing from his own house in a state of serious embarrassment.

That morning Ameda felt happiest merely the sun had risen, and he hadn't died in his sleep.

The Emperor's nosiness and paranoia disturbed Katreina. He ordered all the knights' gifts be ransacked and checked for explosive liquids, live poisonous cobras, and pornographic or violently forceful letters. To everyone's bafflement, there existed no such menace within the heap of gifts. She was allowed then to rummage through the symbolic junk, six piles of it meant for her prior perusal so she could remain stone-faced before her suitors and their families.

Katreina asked herself a question she thought perhaps the knights should have first thought themselves. Why try to impress royalty with displays of riches? Surely this would be a sign of their unanimous stupidity. But there was one gift that stood out from the rest: an encased tube of a fine rolled-up horn rarer than it might fetch for gold. Were there poems inscribed onto the pages? Paintings, perhaps? No, there was not one smear of ink, smudge of wax, or splash of paint. Whoever's gift this was must have been some down-and-out mischief maker. By whatever did this poor, poor knight hope to signify? Pages of horn, not yet written upon, like the vastness of the Myrrh Lake and its unexplored depths, pages if appropriated into a calendar would take her to her deathbed, or beyond. This gesture spooked Katreina – had there been a spy in the bath, someone with a counter-weight against her very real, paralyzing, and naked uncertainty?

She walked away from the gifts to overlook, from an unadorned balcony, the banquet garden and remembered how it was wilder when she was a young child. She mused about climbing a particular cherry willow tree that had later been struck by lightning, turned the color of obsidian, and removed at its roots.

The Emperor ordered a great amount of the space be bricked over so now the design of the garden was in the shape of a canoe, traced with burgundy hedges, dissected by a wide bleached-brick-aisle where chestnut blossoms had been gathered and scattered after a light rain so the pink and white petals might stick to the bricks – and to either side of the aisles six long granite tables rested upon a system of washed-out tangerine colored bricks, so that from her vantage, the garden appeared to be some kind of butterfly or moth creature, and that within the hedges were chopped down pine trees split-in-half and lied down in a cross-thatch pattern, as if somehow Katreina were at once entombed within this creature's cocoon and outside of it.

A chair of ivory and gold elegantly awaited her at the far end of the chestnut-blossomed aisle. And all this was empty, without human inhabitants. She rested her elbows upon the chipped-paint rail and then her hands relaxed across her bosom and her chin relaxed atop her hands as she gazed upon the creation of anonymous architects and masons.

"What is this, now?" she said, having returned to her sleeping quarters to apply her favorite perfume, whereupon she discovered a seventh gift, separate from all the others.

A wooden box, a jewelry box. Non-descript, recently crafted from the smell of fresh fine sanding. When she opened the lid of the box, which slid for it wasn't connected with hinges like a hotel trunk, there were two items neatly distinct from one another: a sealed letter with a black silk ribbon, and beneath this, an unfinished Portrait of the Fey.

The portrait sketched the long legs of a woman, leading into her abdomen – her hair was visible, but her breasts, canvas-colored white, were absent, undrawn, likewise with her face. There was a brilliant, iridescent sweep of color upon her sleeves, which were upraised as if to hold Lunus within her fingertips, but otherwise the only color was from the charcoal, and even these strokes were faint, as if drawn there by an accidental dusting.

She quickly and greedily dug her nail beneath the wax and the letter clicked open. Her heart flapped inside the chrysalis of her chest. How did he accomplish this most impossible of tasks? He was poor! Wasn't he? There'd be no way to bribe even the lowliest, least-paid of handmaids or disgruntled of armed guards.

Katreina's hands shook with the letter resting upon her lap, for she found immediate purpose to sit down – she was blinking back tears of pure ecstasy. The letter, while short, was succinct and demanding: "Three days from now, when the moon is cut in half, find me at the Southern Stables, outside the city, and return this portrait to me. Our imagined kiss is my only truly joyful memory."

And she reexamined the black wax seal in order to assure herself it was his—for as with any other work of art, the artist hadn't signed either the portrait, or the letter. Katreina covered her mouth with her fingertips. Of course she would meet him, and perhaps escape –even for a night– her feelings of imprisonment. She may even give herself to him should the opportunity arise.

What a sweet-talker, a romantic wild man with no manners, his manhood must be the size of all three towers stacked upon the other – the nerves, the guts, the audacity!

Yet, Katreina was needed in public when her desire was for seclusion. Her costume – a dark shroud that became a puppet-like kite, awaited her, along with guests to the banquet garden reserved for a perfect one hundred and twenty, the company of six competing landlords who were ignorant of the futility of their efforts. Worthless half-witted bullies, she thought, tasteless, sex-craven, and greed-stricken fools.

At noon, she donned the shroud over top a silk white dress – she would remain bare-footed until after her performance, and applied a crimson eye-shadow the shroud's hood would cover until thrown above her head, taking flight in the slightest breezes.

After her dance, there were still hours and hours and hours left of social- interaction to combat, and she would be forced to commingle with suitors and their mendicant-faced families.

All the guests seated simultaneously. Ameda and nineteen men under his order, sat at the tables nearest to the Emperor and Empress, who, at a table to themselves were at the opposite end of the white-washed brick lane, from where the shrouded princess would make her appearance.

Food and drink were already established on obsidian dishware – uncooked salmon, rare t-bone steaks, thinly-sliced, with a mound of ocean-colored grapes, and in the glasses, a blackberry brandy – and taking the lead of the Emperor, were permitted to feast immediately. The order of events was this: having received the gifts, the Princess would beckon for the givers to stand and introduce themselves before all others; and thereafter, an orator, on a vassal's behalf, would reenact a poem, parable, or song intended to supplement the significance of his gift. Her shroud protected her reaction, and she did not speak.

These men, with their sad ideas for gifts and lack of taste for poetry, song, or story worth a seconds consideration, could barely enact applause from each other, and the highlight of the evening thus far had been the coffee-encrusted venison with goat cheese and loaves of bread infused with maple molasses, that meal joined with gin and juicy grapefruit pulp. Very well and good – now she could dress head to toe in ghastly jewelry and learned a smattering of art that, if she were to gain power, knew to annihilate from her empire.

At first Ameda felt excited – his gift would have been the last of the evening, and everything he'd done and intended would distinguish himself from this lackluster herd. For example that he was without family, or that instead of relying on an orator, he might project his voice to her himself.

But Katreina skipped him all together. Even the Emperor was not so drunk he couldn't count and when he attempted to protest she held her fingers to her lips and spoke:

"I am graced, my lords," and when she spoke, it was the wind that rattled the grapes on the vines tracing the garden and carried her words ringing round the rims of the obsidian glasses. And she stood from the ivory chair and stepped forward, her face and feminine form obscured. "Now allow me to grace you in return."

Katreina's words so punctuated summoned percussionists from both sides of the chestnut-blossomed aisle—they pushed giant tubs of drums and they began with thunderously uniform, slow beats, one perhaps every five seconds; she seemed to be a phantom, the way the shroud hid all aspects of her human body. Her dance started slowly, too, with the hood raised and her face all dark.

At first, basic ballet, only interpretive, and gentle: She seemed to be speaking with souls, or imaginary friends, or princesses of the past, for she gestured as if exchanging champagne glasses, tipping the air as if toasting, linking arms, and embracing naught but emptiness. It was maddening and beautiful, frightening in so far as she was accurate, knew intimately the widths and heights of other bodies, and the mockery of it all, how the 120 guests each were perhaps depicted there along a predictable path of their highly-mannered behavior, so polite and so perfectly well-rehearsed. She bowed, holding her breasts, as if caught by surprise by an extraordinarily witty joke. This dance, this act, this routine: Somewhat cynical and somewhat comical, at once calling attention to the pretenses of royalty and relieving herself of these pretenses. Katreina seemed to touch each guest this way, from one end of the white aisle to the other, returning where she started, facing the ivory and golden chair.

And all changed, then, when in one striking motion, the shroud at the end of two ninety-foot scarlet ribbons attached to her wrists, rocketed above her head and came to a life of its own.

Clouds as dark as soot arrived inexplicably, rendering the shroud, as if a supernatural servant of death, invisible, only to become visible again as the clouds above turned from dark to white, when there came another source of wicked percussion, from the sky, in the form of hail stones which were smaller than grains of rice. When the first hail stone fell upon the drum, she, a blur of white save for the crimson ribbons around her wrists and the crimson around her eyes, took off at a dead sprint away from the shroud, and it beat back and flapped. The crowd gasped and applauded, for she rescued their nerves from the numbness of drink.

Across the Mirshan Empire, word traveled that Katreina, princess and future bearer of the heir to the throne, was struck through by a sudden flash of lightning.

It had been amidst a dance, and that after the lightning strike she appeared unharmed; it was whispered her insides were transparent, she'd become a dancing skeleton, blinking between this existence and some other; that the Emperor fell upon his knees grief-stricken, not realizing she was still alive.

Was it a light trick—an illusion? A part of the performance?

She enchanted an entirely speechless gathering of men and women and had frightened a few children. She set her feet into a pair of slippers. She took her rightful place upon the ivory and golden chair. She let pass the events of the evening disinterestedly and silently, taking after her father.

Just as soon followed the whispered word of her vanishing.

VIII.

Hustling from the shores of Ri'shurai to the second steppe of the city, his mind reeling and calculating, there was Brayhem with a leather pack hoisted upon his shoulder. And in the pack was a wooden box. And inside the wooden box was a rosily-brown braid, bound with a black silk ribbon.

The Coyote ordered a meeting with his apprentice Makaila at a wheelwright's warehouse and docking station in the northern district, at the moment when Solus's claw relaxed behind the horizon.

Makaila waited. His bony form was like a silhouetted dangling chain.

"If you're high, don't get high," the Coyote said, his yellow teeth clenched and half-visible.

"Where is Isabel?" whimpered Makaila, following behind his master, as they entered the complex.

"We got lots to discuss, but first things first: how fast can you prepare to travel?"

The young man cleared his throat. "Now, I suppose. I could be gone now, if you needed," he said proudly, but obediently.

"Good."

The warehouse, though empty of its workers, held the air of being recently occupied. You could smell the sweat and lifted dust. Coyote lit a lantern and carried it by an iron ring.

They passed benches with half-finished carts, others in need of repair, burlap canvas for wagons, wheels without spokes; and all the tools, ranging from mallets to hammers and saws, were attached to shelving racks. Yet there was, despite the feeling the heat of the workers, another sense the place had been permanently abandoned and clouded over. Coyote led Makaila to a door, and this door led down a sturdy stone staircase into the cellar. Rather small, mainly used by the wheelwright's bookkeepers to track income and accurately pay taxes, both to the criminal organization and the Empire. On the floor, Brayhem lay down a crudely-drawn map of the Mirshan Empire. "We're here," he said, tapping the map top and center. "You'll be stationed here until further notice," and indicated the top left corner.

"Piraz-dai. So near to Ataraxia and the Palace," said Makaila quietly, feeling his heart ring with a tinge of fear and excitement.

"Knowing you can't ride a horse, I'll provide transportation there and back, with six months worth of money to live modestly. This is vital. You break no laws, not even a dog and bear fight, you hear me? You are to remain unseen, unknown, awaiting my fucking orders. Do you have questions?"

"What about Isabel?"

"Listen to me, now. If you told me about her, she'd get our protection. What if she'd been caught? I'm not angry. Ill consequences that might befall her wouldn't hurt me in the slightest. She'll be with you. Don't worry. She's become necessary, in fact. Now – if she's in need of *sol*, I'll send someone to hook you the fuck up. Don't purchase anything of questionable legality. Is this clear?"

Makaila nodded, and, thinking of Isabel, he smiled, his cheeks burning roses.

"Now I need you to perform a favor. Close your eyes, and trust me."

"Why?" asked Makaila, suddenly worrying he'd been set up to be assassinated over his secret love. He backed away, apprehensively.

The Coyote said, "Simply have trust," and when the apprentice closed his eyes he began tearing up in the corner of his eye and trembling, for fear of being stabbed or asphyxiated. Brayhem, with a kind of ether on a dirty linen, clutched Makaila by the back of his head and forced him to breath in the intoxicating vapor.

The boy's eyes fluttered and his body became limp dead weight. He slouched in Brayhem's arms. The Coyote let him down gently, quietly, beside the lamp, so as not to harm him. In the corner of the cellar, beneath a black cloth was one of Rivyn's magical worm-hole chests. He opened it, dragged it toward the lantern's brass light, and then, heaving Makaila into his arms as if carrying logs to a fire, threw him inside head-first – when Makaila's body suddenly disappeared.

As Makaila awoke on a stone floor, his head ached inexorably. His vision blurred, distorted. Yet, upon inhaling, he smelled her, his lover Isabel, and realized she was with him, inside the nest of his arms, asleep and faintly breathing, her snores like sweet sighs. Behind him a trunk was closed, and a padlock shined like a pail full of sun-spears.

A draped window and another of the four palely indigo brick walls. He slid from beneath her and struggled to stand. His knees wobbled and he felt nauseous, at any moment about to retch food he hadn't eaten. He opened the drapes wide and took in the vista of the only other city he'd seen apart from Ri'shurai.

Ameda managed to distinguish himself from the other suitors, the high-minded vassals with no hands dug into mundane dirt, men who would make ill leaders having no sense of the struggle of an every day common civilian, and meanwhile, Katreina's abduction gave him a rare opportunity to prove his worth, and win the favor of the Emperor and Empress, therefore their support should rescuing the Princess help him seduce and wed her.

But there was a problem – having no explicit or immediate participation in the actual kidnapping, he possessed not the slightest idea of her whereabouts.

Rivyn demanded gold and jewelry for the information, and future immunity for crimes of theft within Piraz-dai.

"Back to work I see," said Ameda to Rivyn, who, wearing black linens and no hat seemed to him like a sad funeral director, except that he was busy behind the bar with an older man who was kissing up to a younger man, gossiping about this or that; they were using names unfamiliar to Ameda and his irritation at being ignored grew like an intense fire. He stepped closer to the counter.

"Size matters because shape matters," the older man said. His gray horse shoe of hair he let grow half-way down his spine. "This chap here ain't hung like a horse, but he is carved like a bull horn!"

"Rivyn?" said Ameda. The thief grinned crookedly, his eyes becoming gray and blank, his pupils dilating.

"Excuse us," Rivyn said to the gentlemen. "If either of you need another drink I'll be right around the corner." Then he beckoned for the Night Guard Ameda to follow him to where the kegs of beer and barrels of whisky roll in and where crates of fresh fish are stored for a few hours before consumption. The air smelled like recently baked bread. "I thought I told you about unwarranted intrusions. I'm not uttering one more word to you until you secure my payments."

"I can't pay what you ask," whispered Ameda. "Not for the information, only in relation to what I can actually produce. Expensive commodities go missing from my house, there are countless others noticing they're gone."

"Evidence, Ameda," Rivyn said, patting the Night Guard on his shoulder. "Burn the paper trail. Find me here tonight just after closing. If you're short, my information will be vaguer than you'd like."

"Precisely which keys do you think I own?"

"You're the captain of the Night Guard."

"And this gives me monarchal power?"

"In your station it should," said Rivyn and greeted three new customers, young pretty girls meant to dance on the eve, who decided to imbibe the spirits to loosen their tongues and limbs and relax their nerves before the performance.

The evidence locker would have at least one officer guarding the shack, and a couple of others holding prisoners over night: men who passed out or fist-fought and needed rest to consider their foolish deeds, if they could remember them. He would be forced to relieve the regularly-stationed guard of his duty, allow him to take a walk. Eat dinner with the family, or knock back a couple of beers. Maybe he'd even push the guard towards Rivyn's pub (not that he owned it) so as to remind the thief at any second he could betray him, even implicate him in Katreina's abduction – but if he had the least shred of proof; at the moment, any accusations against him would be unfounded.

Ameda unlocked the back door of the holding jail and entered silently, neither a scrape of his boot upon the floor, nor a jingle from the keys on his belt. There were so few major thefts in the last thirty days Ameda began to sweat. He remembered a money changer reporting a robbery, but could have sworn the coins had been returned by now; he hoped not.

He rummaged through crates marked according to districts; in his haste he forgot if they were sorted by criminal or victim, though his initial instinct toward the former turned out to be correct. Junk, junk, junk. Drugs, paraphernalia, drugs, junk, junk, junk.

And such poor lighting!

He squeezed his eyes and figured he could use a splash of water in them, how dry they became, like glass against a desert gust. No way could he find this amount of money, unless he stole it himself. He slammed shut a drawer that contained a vial of poison and a few arrowheads, snapped from their shafts. He reopened the drawer slowly and contemplated murder.

"Lt. Oriv," Ameda said, entering the main station through the front door. "At ease. I have a few questions in regards to Hinley the currency-changer's case. Have we paper work on the thief – I'm wondering if it's his first crime, or if there are others fitting a similar pattern."

Lt. Oriv, a young bull-headed man with red-tan skin and beard, long reddish-black hair that, even tied behind his head, covered his ears. "Why? Other thefts reported?"

"Yes, only in Ataraxia and within the time frame that our convict has been under Piraz-dai's supervision. Another currency operator is why I'm curious. What if we nabbed the wrong man, the other at large?"

"You suspect a possible repeat?"

"Yes. The one incarcerated took the fall for a thief of greater value."

"Organized crime is quite down, sir, but … our scribe takes care of the confessions, he probably has a written account of the one you're looking for."

The money-changers shop was a red-bricked, one-story cottage near the foreigner's district. So far north, this town attracted sailors from across the Lake of Myrrh, not to mention other seedy types run afoul of the law and carrying the coins of another country. He knew from the confession that less than a grand's worth of silver was kept in-house, for the rest that exceeded a thousand he moved to a more secure location.

No magical alarm system or cantrips set at the door or window, but he prepared for a guard or maybe a dog. The confession admitted to knowledge of an empty hovel under regular protection from regular patrol police. On any given night, the guards might miss the district, seeing as the gates were heavily guarded and all that presumably needed to be guarded.

Ameda approached the front door of Hinley's shop and found, through a side window, it was chained and locked from the inside. Around back, expectedly there was a cellar panel door and he jiggled it to see if it was also chained, but he didn't know, his hearing became clouded; around the front side of the shop, the door opened, accompanied by a distinct metal clanging against stone and dirt. Someone had been inside. Maybe a thief, or Hinley the money-changer. Ameda crept alongside the brick building. Streets away there was so much business left, especially in the pubs. He reached for his leather sap and touched upon the knife. He felt desperate and cornered and knew his chances for redemption from the viewpoint of his family relied on knowledge of the Princess's whereabouts.

He didn't stop to consider if Rivyn's information would be accurate, only he figured his leverage against him should have been such to obtain anything of that nature he wanted, but Ameda feared Rivyn's connections; anyone skilled enough to infiltrate the Palace of Mirshan Empire deserved respect.

Ameda stuck his nose around the corner and Hinley stepped through the door frame. "Hinley!" spoke Ameda. "The man I was looking for!" The man turned wide-eyed as if startled, but then smiled, relieved, though obviously in a hurry.

"Ah yes, Captain Ameda the Fifth. The man I least expected to come across. What can I do for you?"

"Allow me to be straight-forward. I need a loan from you."

"Loans are not my typical business," said the man, wiping his bulbous nose anxiously, waved his hand left and right. "Is it police work?"

"We suspect a thieves' guild is trying to establish itself here, but there's a vacancy as to who is hiring the thieves. I didn't know who to turn to."

"You need a loan to set up a thief?" asked the elderly man. Suddenly he seemed too interested and too compliant, as if trying to keep the attention upon the Night Guard. "I'm sure he worked by himself, though I do question if you got the right guy."

"It's too neat of a confession."

"How much money are we talking? What will I get back?" asked Hinley, scrunching his nose. He had gray bushy eye brows which sweated subtly, and wore clothes unbecoming of his wealth.

"Two thousand five hundred worth of gold."

"I don't have that much of anything here," he said, with a pang of dismay upon his wrinkled face. "Not for tonight I hope."

"Afraid so."

"How much choice do I have, Ameda the Fifth?"

"Next to none," answered the Night Guard acidly. His fingers felt the hilt of his knife.

The man looked to have swallowed a gulp of harsh liquor. "Are you staying at the estate, or a hotel?" Hinley slouched his shoulders and looked away.

"Above a gentleman's club, where the meet is going down."

"Then I'll drive a cart over. It's too great for us to carry ourselves."

"You'll be reimbursed," said Ameda. "As long as you keep quiet."

"In full – Plus, I hope."

Hinley made good on his promise. He tied his horse to a post with the horse's mouth atop a trough of warm water, and ordered himself an ale while outside, Ameda emptied the cart of four, seventy-pound nondescript chests. He felt unobserved. The coins were of the northern currency. In his way, Hinley was playing into Ameda's cover story (thieves operating against governments using rogue currencies, even if these currencies are drugs); and in another way, profiting, knowing these foreign coins would find their way through his shop again.

None of this pleased Rivyn, however. "With all due respect, Night Guard," he said, scooping through these foreign metals. "These are as good as stones to skip back across the Myrrh."

"It's what I could get."

"And poor Hinley! You brought him right to my door step. Now I can't even change them in this town."

"It's the best I could do," said Ameda. His face began to flush and burn angrily.

"Ugh, it's a shame, it really is. The Princess is hundreds of miles away, to the east," whispered Rivyn, his breath smelling like a stripper's perfume.

"That's it?" spit Ameda. "That's all you have to say? Not one name, anything else?"

Rivyn plucked a pipe from his belt pouch and sniffed it, then extended it to Ameda.

"I don't smoke."

"And I don't have fire."

"Then?" and Ameda took a hold of the pipe and dipped his nose into the reservoir. "Faintly of an orange – an opiate."

"Where would that be from?"

"Dream-tear City?"

"Where do they get their drugs?"

"Ri'shurai."

"Yes sir," whispered Rivyn. "Now. That is all, until you come up with funds I can spend quickly and without all this hassle and scrutiny involved." And already Ameda was figuring upon how he could spin a story at the barracks to replace Hinley's loan and realized how easy that would be and how he should have begun there first. It's so plausible, he thought, and he'd sown the seed about his suspicions concerning the growing thieves in Piraz-dai. He rested at home, then, and felt well.

In the morning he'd get Hinley's money if he had to obfuscate the books himself, and discover the name of the crime organizations in Ri'shurai, and whose dominion might reach eastward into the Empire.

Through the Night Guard's barracks, the royal family released a reward for Katreina's safe return, and listen to how much they offered: Fifty thousand coins worth of the Empire's treasury, and rights to a sizeable territory; this note the Emperor signed himself.

When the parchment landed in Ameda's hands, he immediately took leave of his station and made appointment to counsel with the Emperor's viziers, who would likely cover his expenses should he hunt down the kidnappers, and hoped for an advance toward the bounty. He in fact received one, in the form of a rare scepter.

At that time the Palace of Mirshan was infested with the Dark Horse Company's elite soldiers, and it was rumored a demonologist had been summoned and walked furtively among the throng of investigators and other armed forces.

When Ameda arrived at the front gate, his horse was housed at the Southern Stable of Piraz-dai and he walked a couple of miles only to be searched from head to toe, his chest plate inspected, and his black iron helmet pried and probed, his heavy boots dug into and his pockets turned inside-out. The wait to see the Emperor accrued to three months, but when Ameda asked to converse with an advisor directly relating to Katreina's absence and with an offer to help, hinting he possessed a lead but not giving too much away about his information, the Dark Horse Elite hurried him into a meeting.

In the great hall of the palace, the public part anyhow, a balcony could be accessed by a wide set of steps, climbing only eleven feet up, and gave way to the offices of bureaucrats and supervisors of maids and the like.

Ameda wore battle gear, and with his solid reputation was allowed to retain his sword at his hip. The dark circles under his eyes deepened for he lost sleep, and his hands trembled from a lack of alcohol. The vizier, an old deeply brown-skinned woman with long flowing hemp-like white locks, wearing a neat modest violet dress and wooden clogs, welcomed Ameda into her office.

"What's the source of your information, Zaer Ameda the Fifth?"

"I'm the highest in command of the Night Guard of Piraz-dai; there's been an increase of Sol-trafficking in town; Sol is a foreign, highly illegal and addictive substance. In trying to destroy its presence I learned of thieves banding together. Obviously there is no honor among thieves; I caught one, and was informed of a bunch of others."

"A thief's information isn't very reliable," she said quietly.

"Obviously. But if it's between living and dying, we humans are predictable in that we seek self-preservation.

Quite flatly I broke the rules when I started to torture him with small doses of scorpion venom."

"Information gained from torture is even less reliable. He may have admitted to being born from bricks or fairy dust. You put those two together, thief under torture, and the outcome, the output, the consequential blurting out of a ludicrous tale reveals 'truth' to you?"

"Have you received a ransom letter? My supposition is she isn't dead, nor run away which we both know she's done in the past."

"In fact we haven't yet, and the Emperor believes she's alive, too."

"It's logical that, if she hasn't run away…."

"The Emperor feels this is the most likely situation, however, and that she's used her wealth for cover, to escape notice."

Ameda's mouth dried. He felt like he'd swallowed the rib of a fish. "It's only based on what this criminal said, with the highest of convictions, that made me think you're meant to believe she has simply run off. The timing of it, you understand? So young, with so much of her life out of her control, and fifty years or more into the future."

"On the other hand, sir, there's a reason for the extraordinary investigative minds collaborating – he, your majesty, isn't denying the possibility of an abduction."

"I'm suggesting a combination of these two scenarios."

"That she exited the castle of her own volition, and then someone abducted her, the fortress being too secure to infiltrate."

Ameda nodded and exhaled loudly, satisfied his lines of thought were clearly articulated and out in the open.

"I shall then forward this 'insight' to the Emperor."

"Immediately. And tell him I suspect he'll receive a ransom letter and a list of demands within seven days. That meanwhile, I'll be scouring the city for the message's potential sender."

Three days later Ameda found Rivyn and gave him a titanium scepter from the Emperor's treasury he received to track down the Princess and her captors.

Rivyn leaned against the gray brick wall of the pub smoking and staring vacantly into town, its squat houses and chimney smoke intermingling with low-hanging dark clouds. They simultaneously felt the temperature fall and anticipated a thunderstorm.

"You'll need to be acquainted with expensive jewelry. The criminal guild holding Katreina is debating between taking the easy money for the reward, and delivering a demand for a ransom. There are two men you should concern yourself with; they are sons of the guild's leader, but I suspect their business is legitimate. However, they owe allegiance to their criminal father, and with a legitimate business, they have access to storage cells well out of view of either the guards, or unaffiliated thieves. I hope you and your men are willing to get your hands dirty. If my information is correct, they are holding the Princess in a sewer tunnel. She is likely blind-folded, her mouth full of wool, and allowed herbal water only. There is a legion hall for war veterans across from a gambling hall, in Ri'shurai. The sewage access closest to her position would be behind the legion hall, heading eastward. I'll expect half of your monetary gain, Night Guard. If you pay me, I'll move on, and we'll not know one another. If you want to earn extra with the Emperor, follow the jewelers to their father and apprehend him; that is why you've been given this scepter, I suspect."

Ameda thought to himself. He would need nine or more men, and perhaps thrice this many in reserve in case he met violent resistance. The bounty for the conductor of the abduction would provide sufficiently to pay the men, considering their oath of obedience to the Emperor, and to himself.

The first few raindrops were like mist; he felt the raindrops fall, but they didn't wet his skin.

Two weeks of travel.

Their ransom would be delivered by then, and the Emperor struggling to keep her alive, demanding the nigh impossible proof of her continued life. How could anyone take such things on faith? He no longer believed Rivyn, but the fact remained the Princess was missing, and Ameda had his hand in the scheming.

Furthermore, Ri'shurai's sick reputation lent credence to Rivyn's information, he only wished he could verify it. For example, was the Princess in Ri'shurai by now, or en route? She may have been in a dark room in Piraz-dai, or any of the lower districts of Ataraxia, but in either case the inquisitors would have discovered her; this left only a few logical possibilities. She had been killed. Or she had been transported to any one of hundreds of other inconspicuous countryside towns or villages. Or Rivyn's information was mostly accurate. Ransomers get no money for returning a dead princess and at this point in her life, motives to assassinate her would seem negligible. Word traveled too quickly for Katreina's recognizable face to remain unseen, especially since the reward offered would force townsfolk to be extra scrutinizing of strangers. She would invariably stick out, same with her captors. Ah, he thought, maybe the details would be off – not a sewer, but another warehouse, pub, gentleman's club, a drug den, anything. And if she were not en route, how would she have gotten to Ri'shurai within the blink of an eye?

Exasperated, with sleep a kind of strangling phantom weighing upon him, he stepped beneath the awning as rain slashed through a thin mist. Rivyn blew an O of smoke, grinning and scratching a patch of skin at the base of his goatee that Ameda thought seemed scaly, like snake skin.

All Rivyn said was, "If I intend to profit, then why would I lie?"

And this was an adequate explanation for Ameda the Fifth; it allowed him to straddle his horse, pull up the hood of his cloak overhead. He nudged the horse to a slow, mud-squooshing gait. He directed himself toward home, a slow sinking shadow in foggy copper half-light.

IX.

In Piraz-dai the arrival of the Dark Horse Company's inquisitors disconcerted the civilians. They worried over their future heir. Although high politics were not the obvious and most prominent concern of bartenders, jewelers, and clothiers, living in a monarchy meant laws were subject to change quickly between leaders, and the current lineage was benevolent, therefore people began to fear who might replace the Emperor should Princess Katreina had been killed, since Felicity was now too old to give birth without serious health complications to herself or a child.

The Emperor and Empress's popularity revolved around the romantic background of their union. Katreina was born of love, and in fact two years before the Emperor seized power, the main complaints about them were too high of taxes enforced too strictly by greedy landowners, punishments too harsh for petty criminals and, despite beheadings, public torturing, and hangings, not harsh enough punishments for capitol criminals.

Food was abundant, the security of the cities from warring invaders at a steep plateau, and there were rumors of an open alliance forming with northern countries to help oppose the war-mongering rich lands of the west. Piraz-dai, a few miles from Ataraxia (which housed the Imperial Palace), was one of the wealthiest on Aerth.

But it didn't seem so to Makaila in his first few mornings at the Inn of Autumnal Fire, in which his roasted chicken tasted like a handful of sand wrapped in greasy fatty unseasoned skin, the beer was like rotted fruit with brown brackish water poured into a mug, and the other patrons were grim-faced, somber, quiet men of no regular employment, who talked down to him, when they chose to talk to him at all.

The inquisitors frightened Makaila. They asked him questions he didn't know how to answer. Have you seen this woman? Where were you twenty-one days ago? Are all your belongings legal? Are you from this country? This city? Are you capable of violence? Past crimes? What's your job? And so on.

And after answering their questions as if he were guilty of all the crimes he was vaguely being accused of, they left, figuring him for a sniveling, cowardly nobody.

At this rate of living, Makaila predicted well over a year's worth of money, including nights on the town when neither Makaila, nor Isabel could sleep. The cobblestone streets were of a peculiar color, a washed out indigo taken from the lake shore that on the surface crumbled easily yet contained solid cores, all that was left now. What fascinated Makaila was how cool and soft the stones were to the touch upon his bare feet.

Together they discovered pastry shops and stands whose amused-face attendants sold bunches of withered, sour grapes and heart-shaped strawberries that when sucked on tingled the tongue. A tailor convinced Isabel a certain cotton shawl would allow her to fit into the rest of the city folks, and she adored the diagonal weaves, but the shawl was perhaps too large, dangling down around her waistline.

With a small sum of silver, Makaila paid the keeper of a five-story lighthouse on the northern lake to permit they climb to its zenith short of the flame and together arm-in-arm, shoulder-to-shoulder they stood interminably silent and calmer than the quiet water, as a pair of ships crested the horizon. Meanwhile, downstairs two floors, the keeper—a young woman, playing with her children, awaited their father's return from the docks and she sang whispery lullabies that fell Isabel into Makaila's arms, her sweet though gaunt face pressed against his chest.

When he lifted her chin, she smiled and rubbed her right eye and her sharp little elfin nose, and seemed as though she might weep.

"What did we do to deserve this love?" she asked him, and he couldn't reply, for he hadn't known himself.

Ameda tore a shred from the jeweler's silk navy banner, with a diamond ring and string of pearls design, and gave it to his cohorts so they might identify it upon arrival in Ri'shurai. He intended not to join them for he suddenly could no longer believe he'd given Rivyn a single coin he ought to have saved or donated. To trust a thief one may as well attempt to repel the force of gravity.

Simply in case the information was accurate, he sent his men to Ri'shurai with the exact directions given him. Within a fortnight, he'd receive a reply.

"The owners of this banner will lead you to a man named Komodo, the criminal kingpin of Ri'shurai. You are to arrest him, for he is wanted by the Dark Horse Company in connection with Katreina's vanishing."

When Ameda's soldiers left, he returned home for a nap, and prepared to stalk Rivyn, who assumed Ameda was gullible and traveling idiotically eastward on the main road.

It became time to figure out what this criminal was really up to besides vampiring money Ameda himself didn't own.

The cohorts left at sundown which meant Rivyn would be serving at the pub if he hadn't skipped town by now. Ameda figured the thief would steer clear of Ataraxia, but needed to change his currency somewhere or risk suspiciously lugging it around with him. But if Rivyn decided to stay sequestered in his lodging Ameda wouldn't get so much as a glance at him, wouldn't be able to track, confront, or arrest him. The pub owners were already fed up with his intrusions.

Now Ameda thought dark thoughts. When he told the Emperor's vizier about torturing a man, he'd told a lie he might later turn into a statement of fact.

At the gate, Ameda spotted Rivyn Quo'rath, dressed in black and brown, barely recognizable from the color of night, and wearing a black beret, holding a smoky pipe, speaking to the gate guards, and Ameda went from a walk to a jog to cross his path. "Guards!" he called to the three who were rummaging through Rivyn's belongings. "I'll take him from here," said Ameda.

One of them responded: "But it's a routine inspection, sir."

"Of no ordinary citizen, he's under arrest," said Ameda.

"As you wish, proceed," said the guard deferentially.

Rivyn stood quietly, his line of sight searching the surroundings.

"Let's go thief," said Ameda in a rough gritty voice, and he jerked Rivyn by his elbow. "Now, or I'll cut you down."

"Did you forget your steed or something? Where is your back up? I've committed no crime – show them evidence, then, if you have it, or doesn't your highness require proof?"

The guards turned their backs, walked toward their bows at the bottom of their towers, but Rivyn complied.

"I need shackles," said Ameda, "legs and hands, move with a purpose, gentlemen."

When one guard entered his hut to retrieve the chains, Rivyn kicked backwards aiming for Ameda's knee cap, but Ameda was ready, and stepped diagonally away with enough space to draw his sword. Rivyn was on him by then, he hissed, clutching Ameda's strong arm which gripped the sword, Rivyn's hands transformed instantaneously into something like shadow claws, and he slashed Ameda across his windpipe, ripping open his throat. Ameda dropped to his knees, palms pressed to throat, blood fountaining through his fingers. And Rivyn shoved the Night Guard into the dirt. There the dying man gaped like a blue-faced fish, yanked from the lake, a halo of blood pooling around his bluing skull.

Shadow overtook Rivyn's eye sockets, his jaw unhinged, he was frightened or panicked, and darted through the gate, barreling past a confused and bewildered guard who, before he could protest saw red starlight behind his eyes, for Rivyn had shoved the man's head against the stone corner of a tower.

Ameda desperately tried climbing to his feet and shuffled forward, gurgling, and every breath caused vibrations of burning and his nostrils sucked flat he breathed so deeply, his mouth empty, his throat stickily blood-clotted, his neck raining blood.

The guards embraced Ameda, stopping him, calming him, and vainly attempted to staunch the bleeding.

Out of the corner of his watery eye, Ameda watched half-consciously, helplessly dying as Rivyn's low hunched-over carnivorous form evanesced and became one with the lashing darkness of a night of the moon's absence.

The Coyote descended the sewers via the gambling hall's outback access, and in the tunnel passed a woman, wearing not much more than a white rag around her neck. She dropped a yard of rope at his feet. "It worked," she said.

"You did good," he said, and caressed the soft of her belly, beneath the mother-scar.

Awaiting him in an alcove of the sewer were his most skilled killers. They were torturing their prey.

Nine men, presumably Ameda the Fifth's cohorts, hanged by their ankles in an antechamber rigged with ceiling-suspended ropes triggered by traps that resembled bear traps, except they'd been hidden under a layer of sloshy sewage. One man's stomach they ripped open and the guts dripped profusely, splashing the rust and mold-colored muck beneath.

The Coyote cleared his throat and said with cut-glass clarity: "You will perform exactly as I say so, or join him," and he accentuated his words beckoning for one of the killers' wood-cutting hatchets.

In moments, while still suspended, their faces turning purple from gravity overtaking the flow of blood, Coyote's killers stripped Ameda's cohorts of their clothing and armors, piled their weapons, and counted their coins. Finally the Coyote gave them a moment, one way or the other, to forfeit their lives.

Having tossed and turned the entire voyage cutting south-ways over the Lake of Myrrh, Princess Katreina's eyes shuttered open like the wings of a butterfly. Aurora held the infant in his arms and it cried, startled by the "Land, ho!" shouts above deck, when Katreina took the infant up and rocked her gently saying, "Shh-shh-shh, Shh-shh-shh," and Katreina giggled, her face still aglow and sweaty from recently giving birth, wide-eyed between long, amazed stares at her child and knowing glances at her husband-to-be, who helped cradle their bronze little girl.

The ship careened to port at Piraz-dai, a couple of miles from Ataraxia, the palace, and the great mountain.

Katreina wrapped her up in her cloak while Aurora gathered the luggage, minimal as it was, and grudgelessly walked in front of her and yet with the two of them in his periphery so that fellow passengers would not disturb Katreina and their daughter.

Ahead, off the boat, a young woman named Isabel, gaunt and dark, with long sun-light yellowed hair, held her hand to her eyebrows and stood on her tip-toes. When Katreina inadvertently made eye contact with the girl, she hastened forward and said, "Princess," in a soft, somber voice. "May I assist you in your safe return? It would mean a great deal for me."

And Katreina, a shy smile curling her lips and brightening her eyes, said, "Yes, that would be OK," because she knew she would not be alone, now or ever again.

LOVE, HYPNAGOGIA

Thin as thread, with exquisite fingers,—
*H*ave you seen her, any of you?—
- Edna St. Vincent Millay

Once the boat settled against the shores of a ruined Ri'Shurai, a few other frightened passengers hustled away from the boat, devastated at the sight before them, while Wrayth, feeling sick, draped over a horse named Proficiscor, urging him clumsily forward and then paused, standing upon a rotting dock—that thin horse shivering scared of uncertain footing.

She rode the horse, harsh steps along the Mirshanni shore that, off the great Myrrh Lake, ran dead like a spilled urn into the dead city of Ri'shurai.

Spouter Bay was now a wasteland port abandoned by all but the terminally sick and the insanely brave.

The fisher-people loved the sea and their land so much they remained after the cataclysm of meteorite rain that had, with the celerity of a god's hand, deformed the once-wealthy city.

After the thickest walls of smoke had cleared with the coming of a swift and cool spring, and the much whispered-about Marionettes had vanished into the postwar fog, the fisher-people returned to Spouter Bay to find the wildlife changed in ways ranging from quaint to conspicuous.

Many of the long-armed drunkards reported fish twice the size of its species; others talked of dryland walkers whose gills blew rainbow colored dust, and yet they lived. Seafloor algae learned how to talk the common tongue, while others lay smothered undertow, a lifeless gray like granite. Word of the mill was that beneath the Myrrh await a kraken for the first imbecile stupid enough to cross it. Yet more would spit, from behind their halfempty mugs, about the unnatural omens horrific events like these carry.

Spouter Bay. Run amok by smiling children (playing children!) and fat stray dogs along the docks and kitten cats twining about mongers' sun-soaked legs. The smell of fish is thicker than the smell of ale and sweat, the smell of a good cozy inn on the northern coast, where lights used to shine. In the bloodless cloak that is Mon Od, monsters roamed.

Everyone knew the rumors of the Marionettes, these fiendish shells of humans cursed with the sole belief they themselves were vile vessels, evil through and through, and anything living or dead sharing their visage must be evil too, and therefore destroyed.

The land beyond Spouter Bay was iron clad and Wrayth porcelain wrapped in pilgrim cloth. Her horse was thin and tired. Harsh winds swept clouds into ashen walls: A veil over the eyes of heaven.

Coldness bit the traveler's fingers and cheeks.

It was snowing post-conflagration.

For nourishment, the traveler nibbled oat-paste, the residue having long since been frozen stuck to the corner of her mouth, and tips of her fingers. She slept in skeletal abandon if she slept at all.

The traveler traveling …

The road south from Spouter Bay was hidden as soon as it was drawn.

A colorless curtain careened westward, following the west wind.

Wrayth, slouched atop reliable Proficiscor, pulled over her cloak to shield her eyes. So strong was the wind the horse shuffled forward crookedly against it, through ashen wall.

And there was howling in the darkness.

At the pit of a cellar-sized crater, one of hundreds or thousands, Wrayth huddled close to Proficiscor. She blew a warm air into her palms, into the horse's mane and petted him lovingly.

Nighttime descended.

The invisible moonlight.

She opened her eyes and felt with her fingers the ashen earth.

Proficiscor stood with a stupid look on his face. Wrayth smiled at him and climbed aboard him and the horse set off.

For days or weeks, Wrayth traveled over the gray soot-stricken sweep. She encountered no traders, no vagabonds, no pilgrims. The howling of the wind grew harsher and colder. The weather from above had revealed one time a pale cocoon of a sun that grew gray and died and left the travelers to their bone weary shadow steps.

Had she been followed from the bay?

Another night of bellowing howls.

More nights through the darkness without food.

They were lost in some frightening irreparable way. No sunshine upon them. Blue lights of the moon appeared among the powdery fissures of the vertical earth but disappeared much like the roads.

Proficiscor was not overly excited about the lack of light either and was beginning to grow weary of the failing light and the invisible lightless road.

For a couple of hours per day Wrayth gave Proficiscor a rest from her weight, settled well with the idea of walking. Though the earth was soft and wet, once in a while she wondered if her boots had broken an old skull from the meteorite cataclysm. It made her stomach turn knots.

Wrayth huddled and shivering and hungry in the iron cold with wind sweeping tendrils of ash around them like spider webs.

A small encampment, abandoned hours before, was still warm when they reached it. Its folk hadn't been resourceful. Among those things left, Wrayth could only carry the lantern, which she hung by a rope within Proficiscor's teeth.

Beyond, the horizon and coal-colored jagged mountains.

In the cold, Wrayth dug a pit for a fire, but there was no fire.

She looked behind her. Proficiscor was standing asleep.

Rest, she whispered.

His eyes opened briefly before he slid to his belly.

That night, Wrayth sat by Proficiscor and pet his mane and made sure nothing awful would befall him, her dear horse.

*

Wondering, prayed The Minister.

Wondering about what? answered Wrayth.

How much is real & how much imagined.

What difference would it make?

The world.

What makes you so sure?

Isn't that what you think, too?

Yes.

Why then?

I suppose this: To believe in me, to follow the aches of your heart against your reason – you might believe you're insane, and dismiss the relationship we have. What about us is unreal, or could ever be?

Physical closeness.

In some ways, that is very real.

What do you mean?

Only that you hold me closer than any arms could possibly, in love.

In love? With someone unreal?

Is this the case?

*

Ahead of Proficiscor: the vast sweep of white willows marched just beneath a crooked carmine horizon.

Rocks cackled at the base of a mountain.

The horse seemingly suddenly far away. One stride after another, her boots sluiced through the morning dew. Scorry lifted his head staring about with his crooked eyes. Hairlike grass hung from his lips. Wrayth giggled and when he heard this, the horse stamped his hooves and pranced about like something happy.

Wrayth climbed over him and looked to the mountain.

She clicked her tongue twice and led Proficiscor toward the forest.

They rode through an oaken valley; juniper and evergreens; fields of mold-colored withering wild flowers bent westward in the wind. She smelled the pine tar in the air, the disrobed rainless sky above a milky blue.

Birds darted to and fro, singing with the passion of a psaltery. Many lie hidden in trees, protecting nests of little ones, ones who'd be flying in the future, murmuring of secret worlds.

This is how cold the white willows are. Wrayth's lips and nose suddenly froze into little chunks of ice and snow. Snow fell from the trees like crystalline leaves, leaves fell from the sky like light snow.

A forest floor of butterfly-like flowers, green and white wings flapping, flapping, trees climbing from them like native spirits with ropy strands hanging before their auld bark faces, looking on without eyes.

Beside trunks, shrubs with bulbous fruit nested plumply, frost-like roses, tulips with their lips open caught drops of snow.

The traveler traveling.

Above them the sky was invisible, the forest canopy like cloud cover. Silver brooks hush in the distance; and winding along it, Wrayth said: This will take us down the River of Sleep.

Proficiscor plodded along.

Two days, they traveled without sleep.

They followed the brook southwest. A town rested along the river. Perhaps she could barter passage when a merchant boat ran south. That would be convenient, but difficult, because she had very little to barter.

A gray dawn saw her from the great white forest. Satyr pipes still whispered in the branches far away. Golden light in sharp rods bathed the mountains in the northeastern panorama. White like lather: the willows, and for miles and miles they multiplied.

A small riverport, a colony of cabins and men and women in wool clothing. Wrayth watched them. From that distance they were silent and unreal.

Anyone follow us? she whispered to Proficiscor. Hard to tell, isn't it?

Wrayth looked down at him and grinned. Hm, she said. You're a wise horse, my dear horse. Come come.

She was full of music, full of the song and sound in the woods. It drew a thin smile over her blue-cold face. She was happy to feel the warmth of the sun. Here in town, she'd get a tea and rest her hands near a hearth if the hospitality allowed it.

Check the horse, a gate guardian said. The road was very wide, unnaturally, as if when they settled here they expected a much greater population. But the cabins were few and the road clotted with mud.

Where ye comin from, shore not that them woods? An old man inquired, patting the horse on the head.

The old man chewed straw between his lips, a shovel tucked in his arm pit. Proficiscor was to stay here, at the stable.

Yes. She smiled, and glanced his direction. Very beautiful, she said.

Yer goddamned lucky's what ye is, said the man, patting the horse on the head. They's outlaws all over them woods. Ain't no one even goes in there on count of it.

For a little while Wrayth helped the town folks with little things, like loading up merchant boats (which she wouldn't board), or taking watch over children while the mothers got time off their feet. She helped mend a roof and Proficiscor nervously watched her. Town-children chased him about, and as a result, no merchant boats allowed them passage on account of Proficiscor, and his look of having been harassed, which made him seem dangerous. But in return for her aid, they fixed her a skiff so she and Proficiscor could sail downstream. They warned her about the bandits, the outlaws, and other dangerous folk. She wondered how true the stories were.

One morning, she ate breakfast and thanked everyone she could find and a young boy helped her drag the skiff to the water's edge.

Down river surrendered brown and olive rustic scenery in autumn's wear. Outlaw encampments were many. Farms and cabins nestled in the woods, and an old abandoned town was visible from the river. Red-bricked church and overgrown churchyard; fresh but dying white posies spread over headstones, speaking of recent visitors. Squirrels swirled around knotted oaks. Mud-colored walnuts dropped about wide open. The air too was sweet with the summer honeysuckle and ice-crisp air gliding over ravines and limestone cliff shelves.

Along the river small ashen bears, fearful of humans, swiped at white-belly bass. The rocks imbedded below and beside soft as wet turtle shells, and ancient seeming unmoved by time. Weblike roots clawed from the spongy banks. The trees mahogany and silhouetted, and quivering.

The river cut an arrow through the morning fog.

Clouds hung in steppes, and the sun slipped through like a door opening to a lamplit study.

At night, Coyotes keened near, and the brooks fed the river. Bats came out at dark, picking water mites and gadflies from the surface of the river. Owls cooed like mythical flutists, and the night was a hollow den for fancy lights, beacons of careless campers and bawdy vagabonds.

Children sang wordless songs –until, in the darkness, they fell fast asleep.

And soon they came upon the outskirts of dream-tear. There was a fog over the lantern freckled city as though God had just opened its eyes to it, and had yet to focus.

From dream-tear's northerly road, Wrayth and Proficiscor trudged through the slush one hard step at a time.

Framed by eastern badlands and the sheet black shadowood to the west, they watched as the strange folk of dream-tear stirred, restless sleepwalkers of the night. Lunus lit the horse's tracks behind them, which faded into the nothingness of the horizon. Ahead, she noticed the city hired outriders, but that they were lax and lazy. Even as she hailed them politely in her passing, they merely watched her without words while she and Proficiscor swayed into town.

A flat building lay tucked subtly into the mural walls of the noble sect a hundred yards inside the north gate of dream-tear city, and its doors were open to the homeless, and although the city circle and the other self-proclaimed nobles quietly wished the shelter rested deeper in the city, they also enjoyed the fame and good standing it brought to their home.

Demagogues critical of urban ethics were well appeased, while wanderers wandered there for the offerings of food, and the transient residents provided entertainment.

The fires of the hearth were of a natural magic whose embrace calmed the stirring spirit and stirred the deadened spirit all the same.

The owners, Wrayth found, were a married couple of some infinity. Having inherited the estate through some strange lottery of years past, these two used to clean altars in

Sural-jem while speaking and mediating the poor and hungry there.

Their differences fascinated Wrayth. The man was one uncomfortable with, if not fearful of, death though it must be noted this discomfort or fear derived from an unusual love of life.

His wife and greatest love was as religious as a priest but not very dogmatic. She knew home was in the eyes of her God, who would see her when she passed from this life to the next. He dismissed her faith for himself and she dismissed his agnosticism. Irregardless they shared meals and held hands and watched their guests nightly with eyes for the witness of grace.

Rose said to Wrayth everyone is dancing a healing dance and her husband and greatest love said they are the most graceful people he ever laid his eyes upon. Wrayth understood what he meant. Food changed hands across a bridge of yellow candles and clay dishes and greasy hands and dirty beards and suntanned arms, and there was very little to complain about.

Wrayth rested among the lumberjacks and artisans and homeless, who ate fruit salad with sugared rice. The wine was bold and dark and went well with fresh water. Wrayth broke bread with an elderly lady. She had a big cataract white eye and a lovely shy smile and a healthy appetite. The candles went out with the rise of Solus. Many retired to sleep while others picked up another day of tedium, looking for occupation, reuniting with loved ones, or succumbing to their vices.

The bars were dim, lit only by a fireplace and sparse lanterns.

Wrayth adopted the carnival style, a headdress and mask combination, bells and whistles, and flowing silks.

At the grill chefs pulled out the steaks, the Fire Eaters cooked each in one magical stream of heat before moving on with their sparkling smoke balls.

Tumbling nimble kids with spiky hair and tattoos.

Tents and carts of rainbow sheets and curtains, men and women performing magic speaking pompously as entertainers do and the throng of entertained was no less impressive;

the lumberjacks took halfdays, which is unheard of

little animals roved about in trash bins and waste piles already growing high with mugs and empty casks of wine,

abandoned playing cards,

and clothing.

Cheap jewelry were strewn about like unwanted children's toys.

People fed the elephant.

A gentleman and a lady sitting separately, and they were silent as though meditating. The lady doled out fortunes that deeply moved Wrayth. Wrayth ventured away smiling, into a nearby tent.

This place. All the animals. How do you survive in this cold, cold weather? Wrayth was still sleepy and merely looked at all the animals.

The saddest of all them was perhaps the most majestic too. Lying against the bars of her cage was a slender leopard. Her eyes fluttered and there was but a little whimper coming forth. Wrayth pressed against the bars, clutching with both hands. She looked all around her only a pair of tamers talking among themselves, nonchalantly waving people in. But outside, six dancers were dancing. Wrayth could hear the men teasing and jeering and being like dogs, except whistling.

Wrayth kissed her own fingertips and put them upon the cat.

We'll get you out all right, she whispered. But not yet, not yet. When we do, she added, run south, south east okay? Southeast when we get you out.

The cat lifted her head, looking very tired.

No, don't trouble yourself now, she told the leopard. Save your strength. To the trainers, she called: trainers!

They nodded. Yeah?

When's she on, dear sir?

Sundown.

She turned back and the leopard closed its eyes and seemed to slip into a hard-earned sleep.

Wrayth sighed, feeling sick. The birds could fly away the moment the doors opened. But the leopard, they collared her, attached a leash, whipped her when she wanted something besides what they wanted.

Birds have a freedom of sorts, but these birds may have it better here than in the wild. Could that be true?

This is Chari: What a nice curve at the hip, sweetly outlined by violet silk loin cloth; a leather thong exposed at the back, a leather thong over her feet winding up her calves like two dancing cobras entranced. She swayed, she didn't walk. The kind of lovers, or bards.

She said, This way, and pulled Wrayth by the bottom of her hair. She tugged it gently. She tugged it twice. Come come, she said. Wrayth followed, through muddy alleys of sleepy gray and green military tents. She smiled and Chari smiled too. She bit her lip. There's more, she said. This is the place babe.

this is the place

where Wrayth met Mr Grim.

He wore a bucket hat with a single hole through it.

They passed each other grinning.

He raised both brows emphatically, and his lips shaped as if to whistle. The tune hissed as he went along.

He seemed happy, Wrayth said.

See him tonight, Chari said. If you would like.

I think I would like that.

Inside, there were men without trousers. They stood in the center of the structure, one arm and one leg tied to the pole. Women whipped them with cords, while the men touched each other as the women all around them giggled at their awful facial expressions. Chari held Wrayth by the waist and touched her cheek, took her chin: Might as well sit and watch, she said.

The men were red and black and the entire tent filled with courtesan sweat and the dust of dried cum. Chari took a whip in her hand and wrapped it around one man's neck and choked him nearly unconscious and when Wrayth made a move to leave, the man he said: Watch this. And Chari said: he's a martyr, and broke his neck.

Outside, three men waited at the flap with their eyes bugged out wide. Wrayth checked the man in the center of the tent and his warmth was gone. Piss everywhere. Women were already cleaning up. Others played strange string music and hummed and sang seductively. The men, having seen what they should not have seen, fled the tent, promising to tell no one.

As Wrayth trailed them out, she could not shake the suspicion she had been duped by an illusion. For many minutes she waited outside for the curtain to rise and for the actors to take their bows, but that never happened.

Wrayth stood watching from outside the zoo tent, as the other six dancers joined the ritual. They threw knives at men's hats, the tallest gaudiest ones first and the modest ones last. A great whooping of their hacking guffaws made the women giggle and there the cloaks whipped about like light broken through crystal, for the women had vanished, and left only the doves, white feathers, dresses.

Wrayth peeked into the animal tent and there they all were in one hug smiling wide smiles and smelling of vodka and perfume as they strutted on by. The crowd roared and begged for more but the sword dancers blew fire over the feathers, the dresses, and disappeared once more in a storm of smoke.

Fireworks, smoke, and sulfuric things broke the cloud with dazzling lights and everyone present believed, if for a moment, that the dancers were themselves transformed into pretty little lights and were now rising above all the Aerth.

Wrayth asked them: can you teach me?

We can teach you a little something.

Can I borrow a knife? she asked them.

If you try the trick we teach you.

I will, she promised.

*

Now here's a man who's good at the disappearing act! cried Chari.

This was Mr Grim, again.

A skeleton. A bone picking rat.

You're a Night Guard, right? From out of town, aren't you?

Mr Grim nodded.

I've seen you, he said. Why is that? Where?

Chari said: Shh. Come, now. The leopard is soon on.

Soon? Wrayth whispered. Oh, I will see you there, then. In the crowd. A quick favor I promised someone. It'll be really quick. It kinda has to be.

*

After

Wrayth watched the elephants prance around pretending mice scurried beneath them and they also put on a spectacular water show and the crowd was wet and the elephants were laughing, asking for peanuts. A short man with sleek mustaches balanced himself on the elephant's head and once gave the big girl an itch and was catapulted into a bush. The elephants could breathe fire too and they made mist with water and fire and pranced along nimble as any elephant might ever be and when no leopard came out to save them from the mice, the one elephant's heart failed and the elephant died and when the elephant died the fire eaters became shrouded in smoke and vanished, exploding into doves.

Days gone by sitting in the pubs in the darker parts of nen'tor. Mr Grim bought it all and listened to the local thieves and thugs, cutpurses and cutthroats while remembering in great detail each of their words, all of which were buried in cant, in code.

Mr Grim knew the language, being a sleuth in some distant city. He showed Wrayth how to pick out what was being said of importance, and what was Not Being Said of importance. Mr Grim could, as a practice, record entire conversations and store them somewhere in his memory. Given a day or two of work like this, they would find 'wine dealers,' merchants of Allerous Crown– a thriving spy network– in disguise, and sell them information. Little bits here and there. Mr Grim made money. And he spent it as he made it. Citrine, pebble, Sol, Opey, Range; it's called a lot of things, this drug. It's a small orange rock that burns euphoria into the lungs of its smoker. A whole body experience. Electricity into the bones. Vision wanders. Hair like cold snakes with hot venom. The body sweats from neck to toe.

Everything feels good, said Mr. Grim. This is the place.

She gasped, as if shooting up from an icy river. Oh

Hit it again.

Okay. Later?

You can do it now, if you want. Anything you want.

Where are you? You don't know.

Her skull was a clock winding up. Tightening. There her fingertips quivered, pinched the space above the eyes. Tightening with no way to release, to snap.

Here you are, he said. This is what you want. A little pipe and her eyes opened with orange turning brown and gummy in the pipe's fire. A small tear ran down her cheek, but it was a tear of ecstasy. Tingles in her spine and through her fingers and at the corner of her little mouth.

She nodded, smiling, wiping her hair away.

We've a great day planned, remember?

Mr Grim was wearing a uniform. Mr Grim was unshaven. He smiled. And it seemed to her the like she was at that moment an object of paternal love.

He rubbed his chin and said, Go on get ready.

But Wrayth was ready. She had slept some sort of sleep in her only clothes and when Mr Grim noticed this, he grinned.

We'll take care of it. Come with me, he said.

She giggled, a moan more like and could barely stand. Oh, she said.

We'll take care of everything, he said.

OK, she answered. As they hobbled down a dark corridor, Wrayth realized she knew not where she was. Blue fancy fire smelled like stagnant water lighting the tight hall in a pale milky glow: Mr Grim held her hand but he himself seemed invisible. She followed the dark into the dark and she screamed, empty of air, a gasp so suddenly frightened by something she saw.

What is it now? He pulled her close. It's just down here darling. You'll be okay, won't you?

She did not answer. She walked as he walked.

His step was a shadow step.

From one absence to the next.

Right down one corridor, left through another. All the same, these halls.

Quiet shadow step.

Quiet except for the hum that vibrated his smoky lips.

He looked back to her after a great inhale.

From Darcanna, from nen'tor the new city, they stumbled into the governmental district and attended a dinner there and Wrayth was quiet and comely and batted her eyes at charming princes and she ate nothing. When Mr Grim was finished he said, We have a long night, in a very manly way and the people at the dinner laughed at his joke. Later they visited a slimy wine vendor and Mr Grim bought a wine, although he took a long time to haggle the price of it and when he came to Wrayth, he owned more coin than when he stopped at the shop. This filled Wrayth with excitement.

Couldn't do this without you, he said.

The orange brown smoke cooled her down, laid her down in that nice cozy cot.

Mr Grim gave her wine, one full cup, and said: this is the sleeping elixir. Used to give it to my child, he said.

Days gone by without a thought which did not wrap itself around the drug. Over and under nen'tor, the pubs and the brothels. Seedy establishments smelling of rat fur and filled with the whispers of occult activity and criminal enterprise.

These people: Their teeth were rotted, legs missing, pegs in place. Many wore patches, steel noses and gloves over disfigured hands.

Nen'tor was a city of boils and disease. Illnesses of the mind spread like rumors.

Perhaps chemicals in the water.

Witches cursed the ale.

Nobody seemed to know.

Quack medicine became the rage, and many posed as doctors with experimental but effective medicines; many of these died. They were killed. This is nen'tor. You can't go around cheating people. They'll roll you into a ditch where a stray dog will eat your corpse before it completely rots. Bones and all.

Where do you think the orphaned infants get their rattles? Human teeth.

Over a warm watered down cider people talked of crazy things and picked fights with the chefs and sharpened their knives needlessly. Darcanna, the undercity of dream-tear, was sick.

There are

Out there

In the world

Things which no person can save.

And nobody knows which things.

But they exist, said Mr. Grim.

I don't believe that either, Wrayth argued.

I do not believe that either, Mr Grim said. This is an assertion based on evidence, he said. Science, it is.

Your science is very flawed then, she replied.

Very flawed science? I've observed a pattern. It exists and I've noticed it.

In the question of ethics, she said, can there be scientific answers? Can you say the cosmos have determined what it means to suffer for each individual?

Grim ate a mash of rice while they talked. A bug, perhaps a cockroach, scurried across the table carrying a bit of the rice over its shell. They ignored it.

Grim ordered pork and potato pie. He sat deeply in his seat staring at it. I miss them, he said. Before I'd done the nightcrew down south – Used to be a farmer.

Wrayth was delighted to hear that, but she wasn't sure why.

A bum old man asked for some coin: cain ye give us oner two?

Wrayth looked to Mr Grim and he shook his head.

Finish my rice, she said.

Mr Grim looked surprised and said: you don't want money for food or you'd get some food. Listen old man ask someone else, I'm eating.

Actually I'm finished, said Wrayth.

Mr Grim sighed. Actually I'm finished, he said. OK? Finish my rice. Fine? Now go on.

The beggar rubbed his hands together and he nodded graciously to Mr Grim and when they left she saw him through the window finishing the meal.

Things have changed.

The pursuit of the drug has become intense.

Wrayth cannot control her concentration.

She has spent a lot of time braiding her hair

And unbraiding it

And braiding it again.

This is Millay.

Beautiful and middle aged, secretly a servant of a nameless God. Plain rags and tan skin, or dirty skin. She smelled of vanilla and mint.

When they met, rather than shaking hands, she and Mr Grim hugged.

Wrayth enjoyed her warm personality.

Solus? she asked.

No. She shook her head and pulled back. No, not him.

Mr Grim helped Millay clean the shrine. Wrayth did not recognize the shrine: it was a tree, very stout. Pale and thin, it had grown through the floor somehow and reached toward the ceiling.

Not sure what I'll do when it gets bigger.

Prune it, I'd say. Or chop it down. Does it grow fruit? asked Mr Grim.

Wrayth said, I don't see how you'd prune it though. It hasn't any branches. Just a thick trunk.

Millay smiled. Probably just cut a hole in the ceiling and let it go.

Let it go?

Oh. Well, I feel blessed it's here. What kind of gardener am I if I cut short something so beautiful?

That's an appropriate question, Wrayth whispered. What kind of gardener?

Ah, Millay said, suddenly jovial. She clasped her hands together, her lips pursed sweetly, as people hobbled into the green room. They had with them small purses with small amounts of change in them. They're here to pray, she said. Are you?

Mr Grim said that they would stay, but not very long. They had things to do.

Orange. They were not, as Grim said, present very long.

Indeed, they had things to do.

Millay's shrine must have been on the upper floor or Darcanna, to the east side because as they walked away, the sun was rising– rising and reaching its long mono-white fingers through the slits in the walls, through the shuttered window panes. Long corridors, black but illuminated. Winding away, Wrayth watched as they walked silently through the corridors, toward the deep center of the city, the underneath city Darcanna. The light was at once a candle burning, and a candle fading. It became gray. The color of dust; the color Mon Od. And in moments she could see nothing else.

Darcanna was a labyrinth dragging through caverns below the city. It was built as a garrison to ward against invaders and must have had an infinite depth beneath dream-tear. The districts, as far as Wrayth could tell, were denoted by the different wax lamps set in disparate polarities. Some burned a deep blue, some orange some violet or yellow. Mr Grim said that every year more people descended to find a means of obtaining money. That Darcanna had quickly become a criminal hotspot. Not only for drugs, he said. Smuggling and other forms of tax evasion. We feed the poor, he said. All who find Darcanna anyway. Nen'tor above had no group like those who began Darcanna. A fierce group from where Mr Grim used to live, but where that was he wouldn't say.

I live here now. I know it's difficult to figure, but this place is a place every thief or outlaw in Mirshan dreams about, but cannot find. The people here do not operate above. He grinned. Not often, he said. Well, the drugs you're thinking right?

That's all she could think of.

Smuggling's bigger, he assured her. The people who come here can't afford taxes. Not that this city is unfair. Let's face it, it's decent – Oh my. It's hot, he said suddenly. We need to see my man pretty soon.

You're out? Wrayth asked him nervously.

He nodded. Yes. Mr Grim was sweating profusely. Whew God. God damn, he said.

You said he's a preacher?

Oh. Yes he's a preacher.

Like Millay?

No. She's a servant.

Like we are?

Do I serve God? Mr Grim hummed to himself, wiping his forehead and upper lip. I know of only one, he said. A raccoonlike grin across his bony face, a dead raccoon smile.

It's hot, isn't it?

I'm okay, she said.
Well. I'm okay, he said. Very busy today, but it's okay.
Wrayth followed
from white
to gray
to yellow
And at the bottom
of a staircase
they knocked
*

It starts again, here.
When she woke up and Mr Grim
Was nowhere to be found, Wrayth
Felt a heartache and fell asleep
She remembered the drug in his hands, the kind of hands in which the vessels line the back, thick and green riding along the bones and knuckles. The globe, the bubbling orange pebble. Solus in his palms, smokeable Solus. But the hands were gone, the God gone. Hidden in the shade of the city, Wrayth wept and felt very sick. In her stomach, voices yelled to her. Children's voices, hungry children.

Wrayth visited the privy and there she vomited the bile of a drug-induced sickness. There was no food nearby and so she wandered into the populace, the districts of Darcanna where, beneath dream-tear, there was an open cavern and in that open cavern were the greatest trade-stalls. And the cluttered bars, dirty little brothels full of men slouched in their chairs. Many people wore masks hiding their status as statesmen, merchants, knights, beggars, whores. She wandered. Weird-looking pack animals, like diseased or angry horses and camels, some, within their teeth, held lanterns by rope (while others were dead on the stone) so that the streets had formed from the stringlike lights and became blocked by fiendish guardians.

Men without cause always turn to guarding something, don't they? Mr Grim – What cause did he find or fall for?

The people in the streets were very quiet. Beneath the earth, silent. Hacking coughs thus resounded in the cavern markets, the dry scraping of fleeting boot pads over the cold stone, the firing of torches, and drugs; the blathering of the animals. And the stink.

She wandered among them.

A small stall open with benches. She'd ask around. Where is he? Mr Grim? His spirit could not be reached.

She spoke with a man who called himself The Minister Quo'rath. He looked down and patted his side, crookedly grinning. We just got these, he said. Across the bar he rolled a cigarette. You want one?

She said she did.

He scooted closer, a couple of stools closer, a couple yet away. My boss got them from a merchant. Wasn't long ago.

She turned her head to one side and squinted. She tried to remember. And like a curtain drawing up, revealing the stage and the actors, she remembered him.

You, she whispered. You see me.

He imitated her look of surprise, his eyes gray and blank. Hm, he said, lighting the cigarette. Rathi smoked it, halfway, and offered it to her, but she didn't take it.

They were quiet except to order a small meal. On me, Quo'rath said, continuing to smoke.

When a server served the potatoes bread and cabbage, the man ate the food slowly making sour faces.

Never get used to it, he said.

Can't imagine.

They both seemed sad.

Hey, he said, scooting to the stool beside hers. He said: You seem like a very sweet lady. Maybe you are not.

I don't think I am.

We'll see, won't we?

What do you mean?

He pulled out his change purse, to pay for the food. Why are you here? he asked.

She sighed. I'm traveling.

But when you arrived?

She didn't answer, but she stared at his face. It was hard and yet had fine features. His crooked lips, chapped. A knobbishly broken nose and tightly trimmed goatee. Those eyes, so empty and gray, which brightened when he spoke.

You're a sweet girl, he said. Maybe not.

Millay found Wrayth in the bar, talking to this man.

And Wrayth recognizing if briefly her distorted world for what it was, let her world shatter, when the servant of an unknown deity gave her what she wanted.

Smoke only a little, she said.

Wrayth nodded as she smoked and the warmth of the center of the sun heated her body. She could no longer listen.

You know, she said, then, Mr Grim is doomed to be consumed by his love. If you think that love is you, or his wife, or any children, you are wrong. Mr Grim is not a good man.

He is not awful, though. Is he so awful?

Millay only looked at her, watched Wrayth sigh and smile as the pebble cooked and the smoke filled her body.

They walked away from there, leaving The Minister Quo'rath to himself and his meandering thoughts, through the absolute center of Darcanna, and into the night, when Wrayth left Millay again.

She sneaked away, looking for Mr Grim or his drug dealer. She had no coin and could not do her work without Mr Grim because he knew who to sell to. She knew nothing. And when she did not find Grim, she found his connection, and the world seemed to click back into place, become lucid again.

For the drug, the pebble, she slept with him in his bed and did all the things he asked her to, which were awful, and all there is to be said of it is that she had not remembered them in the way people remember other things. She watched herself, as though through a peephole in the door. There had been blood but that delighted him. It ended without redemption, except in the form of a gummy brown in a pipe and smoke down her throat –the numbing of her body and of her mind. He told her she could not stay the night.

She slept for hours and ate little. The streets were cold. Her dress soiled. At night every night…for how long?

She went back to him, like a battered wife who couldn't leave. Her love was Mr Grim's love. She went back to him and pleasured him and slept on the streets.

When Wrayth found Millay again, Millay said: I'll show you where Mr Grim is. I'll show you what you think you want, she said. I tried helping you nicely. Now there's no time for that.

Wrayth was out of body.

Watching, her eyes sunken and pathetic.

Who do you think these people are? They aren't strong, they're sick, she said. These people are sick, and you were their healer. And you've abandoned them. Don't you understand?

Wrayth and Mr Grim were reunited, but something had changed. Grim was dirty, with coal all up his arms and over his face. The Night Guard hired him on to work in a furnace for a temple to get more money. He looked real bad.

Wrayth wanted badly to find a mirror and to look at herself, to be reassured she existed. There is no vanity drug. She lost herself like one might lose oneself in perfection, or in a lover. It felt good, and its absence was a devastating void. Its absence was her absence.

Mr. Grim had no money.

And no more work.

One night when Wrayth lay restless in her bed Mr Grim came to her door and he said good night and left as suddenly.

She felt the coins in her fingers, thinking of Quo'rath. From where did she remember him? Their connection felt primordial, ancient.

Her body ached for Solus.

Sol

ssss.

It didn't happen. She wanted it badly to happen and it didn't happen.

Everybody was right about him. He left her like he had left everyone else. Men become infinitely harder to please in a world with so many new things. What cause was he fighting for? What new drug. What new lady?

Maybe he died. The monster feeding on him finally swallowed him up. His body lost to darkness, his spirit smoke in an unlit room.

And frightened and suddenly she rose from bed and sprinted out, sprinted past the places she like a ghost had haunted searching for Mr Grim sprinted through the corridors sprinted to that thick pale tree, the secret shrine, and she saw whom she needed to see, a truly loving person, and when she saw Millay lying in her bed by the shrine she clutched her by the cot's rags and fell to her knees –only Millay was now dead. Her brutalized face, splintered elbows, and crooked neck.

*

Wrayth fled from the city of dream-tear.

She tried not to look behind her.

Dream-tear: Darkness closing its fist upon the city.

She hugged Proficiscor about the neck.

The air was cold and clean.

Wrayth kneeled at the edge of a gray stream silky by the moon's low light. She cupped handfuls of water. She splashed her face. She rubbed her face. She waved her hair around to catch the coolness of the wind. She drank deeply. She looked up once before she fell

into a calm slumber

by the River

of Sleep.

Proficiscor woke her with a nudge. Her eyes focused on him, she was saying: What is it?

For his broad face was full of horror; his hairs raised up.

Dawn met her with a cold white hand. She felt pulled to her feet, as though against her will. The aches in her side.

By the stream, she rested, vomited, and the vomit was yellow.

Will you walk? whispered a prayer.

You followed me, answered Wrayth. You see me.

The man named Kapswelle nodded and said, Will you walk?

I will, answered Wrayth. For now I will

They traversed the sparsely wooded plains along the River of Sleep, an hour east of the shadowood. A bitter wind swept through dead grass and unharvested rice fields while the days, though cold, were dust dry.

At night, Wrayth slept uneasily, haunted by nightmares that woke her in sweaty agony.

The poison of those dreams widened her eyes wider every night and it took longer and longer for her fatigue to shove them shut.

By day they approached the shadowood.

Wrayth shuddered and led Proficiscor around prickly roots sticking wickedly from the wood's peat black floor. Fallen over, the trees continued to grow, ashen, in weak resemblance of Solus, who could not penetrate the depths of the interminably dark shadowood.

A sickly smell swung like a sweet milk soured in the sun. It smelled of wet death, flowers in the wood like skulls in the distance, eyes up close, eyes that followed and followed, being led by the only light.

Proficiscor kept his head low, feeling shy, out of place, and silent. Kapswelle walked out ahead of them by a thin path. Wrayth and the horse chanced upon a clearing and in the clearing lay busted fragments of a caravan. There was no sign of a struggle, no blood, no hair, and it appeared it was abandoned, rather than attacked. Foodstuffs still littered about the wet black forest floor. She checked the wood of the caravan and it had for the most part rotted. There, Kapswelle made a fire from the broken bits of wood, and ate of his own food, which appeared to be raw eggs.

From these few sparse trees men manifested like hungry poltergeists.

How quiet were these men, as spiders burrowed in soil, with matted hair and gritty arms. Greasy lips and beards rampant.

Shadows clung to them unnaturally, and the scent of dead animal shrouded the few clothes they wore. Possessing the silhouette of monsters, only two women were among them— and they were armed heavily with blades, nets, and clubs.

Proficiscor inched close, but made no sound. Both he and the traveler sat motionless as the ghosts of the wild came forth.

Now hear that? one announced. Silence, he whispered. What would it be, you think, if there was a man walking incessantly like a lunatic?

I'd think it was nothing unusual, answered Wrayth.

White teeth flashed. A grin like a dead animal skull. Outside the firelight, this man unsheathed a blade.

Perhaps this man is nearby, yet.

*

Of sleeplessness:

Cold drained the world of its color.

Wrayth limped beneath a tree, frightened, her head feeling under severe compression. She imagined the lowlit fireplace of home and the warm stones of those walls and the calm comfort of her reclusion.

Proficiscor, she moaned in a whispery voice, dear horse, where are you? Her legs were crossed at the ankles. She felt paralyzed staring at her muddy boots.

The men were without sclera.

They were white-skinned and full of whiskey and fire and ready for extreme and senseless violence. Bear pelts increase the size of men into monsters. The two women among them, spidering in and out of her sight, vanished behind the veil of monsters, rows of men. New flesh for these lecherous men. New skin to be worn over their bones. New meat to be forced down their gulls.

Wrayth closed her eyes, begging no.

*

The woods were dark.

We are here, someone whispered. She did not sense Proficiscor, who hadn't been captured.

It was the wind, a chorus of throats seeming sunken deep into the trunks of trees. She wrapped tight her hands and arms in gray cloth, so they would not be stung asleep by the venomous thorns of the shadowood.

Bleak shafts of light revealed empty black mud, and star-shaped ivy, shimmering with a vile sweat. It led them through haze, seeming like the inside of God's eyelids.

When the night came the clearing seemed swallowed up whole. The flames a bold tongue licking the gums of the forest. The tops of trees spidery and in constant twitch.

Wrayth did not sleep.

After preparing to move on, she massaged knots from her muscles which had been built by undeniable fear. She could see nothing. And her arms were cold. And her legs were cold. And though then her hands were free, they were frozen around an iron collar set around her neck. It was chained, she learned, having tried to leap away. Her body was bare and wet with black soil.

Where am I? asked Eliza drowsily.

Shut her up. I'm not fuckin jokin, a fellow prisoner snarled. He said, Quiet. Lest they kill you. Close your eyes and try to sleep.

Don't sleep, said Kapswelle.

When they leave, we can talk, he whispered.

When who leave? Wrayth replied.

When who leave? said Kapswelle, then.

Wrayth swallowed what felt like a solid bitter apple. Tears ran down her face and she wanted to run, but the chain was too tight to run any way, except in a circle. They could only trod little ovals; she heard the other prisoners trodding little circles.

We don't know who they are.

They hack us into pieces and place meat into a fire.

Humans, why? asked Kapswelle.

It's a human farm.

The collars and chains tightened about their necks, so they could only roam in circles. Each chained to a separate post deeply rooted into the earth. The humans permitted no physical touch or contact with each other.

A woman named Eliza was pregnant. She became hysterically insane when she considered someone or something was waiting for her to birth a child, to be fed upon.

A certain miller had plans to escape but was hacked into pieces and fed to the shadows.

They take one person a night. There are not many of us left, said one of the prisoners.

And then: Embers flared.
  The blood of humans
  spilled
  gurgling screams
  rippling
  empty space
  uninhibited, unchecked.
Every chirp and moan stealing the prisoners'
Hopes for future life
That was my wife! a man cried, but his face and form
were unknown.

He strangled himself unconscious, an attempted
suicide, a failure.

That's how I should go, whispered Eliza, cradling her
belly. Break my own neck.

Wrayth felt crippled sick, the whole of earth seeming
suddenly up-side down.

They'll eat it anyway, said someone quietly. We have
to escape.

Miller done tried it, said Eliza. Look on where it got
him.

Fires only when they cook; that's what Miller said.
They don't need the light, so it's almost always out.
  And as blood splayed
  from the end of a stone axe,
  over sweating venomous leaves
  pulverizing crushing limbs,
  these living stared into the darkness
  as though aboard a ship at sea,
  waving farewell to a city they once loved,
  and would no longer see.
Wrayth saw seven serpents in the trees

dangling & hissing
& entangled & alive &
twice this many
yellow amber eyes and
forked-tongue-tips of blue fire
Was she dreaming?
Of fire and light,
Limbs in red flesh ribbons
Flesh spit into a dying fire
hissing as the flesh hits sizzling
Rust red demons
quivered kicking up clawed dirt
tearing and rending in their obsidian teeth
human skeleton femurs
red human spines
gripped in rigid jaws
they whirled them impaling them bloodless
over twisted tree stumps
and brokenly crushed broken against stones
the only escape from this prison was death,
but death had fled these prisoners.

Oh goodness, she wept to herself, watching the vilely winged monsters prowl over the kills, sinking fangs into their victims' throats leaving none alive.

None fed on the meat, and it seemed to Wrayth that another hunger altogether had been satiated.

She vomited yellow-white bile into her lap, a trepidation overwhelming her. The coldest winds could not have hollowed her bones quite so.

A demon's wail, as powerful and ancient as a dying star drew blood about her nose.

No. She had not been dreaming, for it was not that kind of sleep.

How had Wrayth become unchained?

The sounds of chains slithering like steel snakes.

And the joyous half-giggle of the demons.

Someone squeezed her arm, tightly to the bone.

Wrayth clutched Eliza, then, and she Kapswelle, and Kapswelle, muttering nonsense to himself, held onto another, a broken down man, and in one line they flowed through the trees, like shadows among shadows –

but in the distance

fires were lighting

and the earth

quaked

Snarls shot out

and slobbering behind them as they sprinted toward vague points of broken bone-colored light;

the farmer fell in a deep deposit of mud; the poisonous thorns stung him like scorpions

and there Eliza had paused, so shaken, still they crawled through the stalagmite trail of black and rotted trees

Wrayth wept silently for the fallen, and yet could press only forward—and they sprinted forward, stumbling often without their bare feet touching the forest floor.

And suddenly all senses converged: the blood in their bodies with the dry Mirshanni air, with wormwood and fig, the cool moon and the sharp cold leaves, and the haunted howl of the demons echoing like a murderous impulse.

*

Besides Wrayth, Kapswelle and Eliza were the only survivors, and together they traveled south. Down a hollow road, Kapswelle agitated Eliza because he paced all night as far as she could tell, whimpering to himself like a dog left without food, and the inner violence of Kapswelle's spirit frightened Eliza, but she controlled her fears of him in equal proportion to the lack of expression of his violence, for she didn't fear *him* precisely; she feared what drove him to sleeplessness and she wondered what shame he might possess in secret.

They both needed comfort.

More and more, they took to walking,

Day and night they walked.

He walked hunched over, his eyes closed and fluttering and he walked rambling incoherent groans like storm clouds that do not release rain.

Do you ever stop? Wrayth said irritably.

Do you ever stop? asked Eliza. You almost got us killed.

Kapswelle shrugged, smiled, and shook his head.

Do you sleep?

No, he said. He stepped into the light of their fire, pacing around it with fast feet.

Is someone chasing after you?

Wrayth wrapped her arms about her knees and said nothing. A blue light bathed Kapswelle in warmth given to them all by the fire heated by the burning wood fallen in forests rooted in the soil which now they stood upon.

Briefly, like a lover's hush breath on their necks, a wind rustled through the trees, rustled rotten fruit-filled leaves, whispered in all the world's ears saying little things of everything; this was when Wrayth and Kapswelle bound souls. She was with him, and would always be with him.

The darkness crept in as the fire died.

In the morning, Kapswelle cooked grubs and insects with mint, walking circles around the fire, and kissed Eliza on the forehead, walking circles around Eliza.

Confessing sins accomplishes nothing and isn't useful, said Kaspwelle honestly and finally.

That's true, Wrayth said and felt apathetic towards him, concerned only with the health of Eliza's child.

That's true, said Eliza. Confessing is a kind of running away, isn't it?

Night fell.

As the wind whipped, she and Kapswelle watched together as the stars turned to dust and flitted and fell into the peaceful black firmament above each and all.

Lunus obscured her face, to observe stars in a humility not oft observed by goddesses.

Starlight, down upon the Aerth, like bedside candles white and blue, some fading some firing to the prayers of the prayers of pain and peace.

Morning found her sleepless, eyes aching and swollen and salt dry.

Solus was slow to breach the horizon. The sky was a lavender blanket of clouds.

The badlands deep in the distance like an abandoned seascape where no shadows crept about its surface, and beneath its surface there was no life.

Wrayth and Eliza and her unborn child ran south until fatigue paralyzed them, and there this gray pale horse haunted the night road.

Where were you, dear horse? Wrayth whispered.

Proficiscor did not huff or stamp in circles. He didn't seem excited or frightened, but patient like a mountain, waiting for the riders to continue forth.

Eliza was with child, and sat atop Proficiscor during the day, the weight of the child in her belly resting in the middle of the horse's spine.

And in their travel south, in search of civilization, they met a young girl plucking grapes by the great River of Sleep.

Her hair was silver and she wore soft silky lilacs and a thick braid.

This girl knew somehow of their suffering and offered to help them, emptying a bundled jute sackcloth of apples onto the river bank, and they ate the apples and adorned the cloth and the little girl led them peacefully to a village, where Eliza stayed.

And about this little girl Wrayth learned she was a curious girl who wandered the villages and the wildernesses at night, communing with foxes and birds and flowers, because she could not sleep.

She explained away the sleeplessness saying, because in this world some people are without food and they starve to death.

How can I sleep when people are starving to death?

THE HOLLOW

Lupus Est Homo Homini
- Titus Maccius Plautus

I am a courier named Mousai.

This is what I remember.

First I unfurl a letter from a knight of the Mirshan Empire. His name is Rozkhe. He lives in Quriah, near the River of Sleep.

The paper is brown and coated with wax. I can smell the ink barely dried on the page. "Take this to Crawing," he says. "It's out of my way. Take this to a gentle sir named Chaw. Can you do it, son?"

For him, and the welfare of Mirshan, I answer yes. "I am honored."

But the first moment I get alone, I read this letter:

Dear Regent Chaw:

The purpose of this letter is three-fold. With war prisoners held in Quriah, the slave owners are anxious to hear who will be hanged. I expect that you have that list ready when my courier arrives. 2 of every 10 of these men will change hands south.

There shall be more slaves than hanged men so I suggest you schedule an auction platform as well. Finally the Imperial diviners inform me orphans of the war are traveling from Somnah City, a day or better ahead of a terrible storm. Raise alarm with the guard.

Apprehend them if necessary, but beware of them.

—-ZAER ROZKHE of DHC, QC. Monsep XXIV

The sky above is molten. Sweat trickles to the edge of me nose and I wipe it away. Could be weeks till we get rain. Or there may never be rain again.

Stuck to the horizon is a great sheet of airy haze, pink like a scar beneath a blurry sun. Very little wind stirs the scalp of the desert, still and dry as a skeleton; there I stand in the quiet rib cage. Ridges like jagged teeth and spire-like ribs shoot from the spine of Mirshan. Only the faint smell of campfire, smoked arbol, and sagebrush sits easy and most natural.

A vulture circles above me— caws, cries. It begs for more war. I sigh, wipe me forehead and pet Priea, me horse. I let her lick meal from me hand. She snickers and stamps her hooves light and playful.

I tug a piece of hardtack from me pouch and stuff it down me throat. Dry like sand, and not much better taste either. But I'm used to poor tasting food. It's just nutrients so I ain't starved and that's all that matters. After swallowing, I look skyward. It's time Priea and I moved on.

*

Sudden tumult. Sudden blackness. I know I dream but I can't remember what about. Whatever inside of me is awake sees a red light fingering through the dark, prying open me eyes. Making room for true suffering to sting and bludgeon me all over.

And what but a man who casts shadows longer than shadows should be cast at noon kneels beside me? This man who is not a man will be called The Minister.

"You are injured and perhaps lost," says he, calm and kinda quiet.

"The pack here found you." His sharp eyes cut me skin.

"Where the fuck." All I smell is ammonia. I widen me eyes and try to look around, through a fog, and see his face more clear. "What the hell happened?" I try sitting up, but can't. Two skinny figures like wasteland arbol wait a couple of paces away. One's eating an apple. I grunt. I bet it's mine.

"For Godsake answer me. How long's I asleep?" Ary muscle sears to the bone as I struggle to sit up. "Where's me horse, zaer?" I say fair loud. "Tell me something, goddamn ye."

The man closes his eyes.

His companions part like window shutters and between em I see Priea lying dead with spears up to her neck. A brown pool of blood swallows her pretty mane. I choke on dust and scramble toward her, dragging me legs. "Ah...no."

Those two men leave me be a moment. "Prakas? No no..." Dust spits from me mouth.

"Come, young pup." The Minister beckons. "Have water, food."

Those skinny men chuckle to em-selves. I can't see em enough to trust em. What if they fuckin did this? "I had food. But a bit of liquor'd do me well. I want then to be on me way. Crawing ain't too far from here."

"Ho, whoa," the guy with me apple says. "You ain't goin nowhere alone, pup. You forget to check his knee, Minister?"

"No," says he who is called The Minister. "But keep tight your jaw, Shiv. He found the injury himself, didn't he? And the pack should nurse him, you suppose?" His eyes open as though inviting an answer. After a silence, The Minister hands me a canteen. I take it. The water's warm and soft swirling down me throat. I imagine there is mud in me gut once I get me fill.

I catch a good look at him. The Minister. His skull shows beneath the skin. Carrying the fat of a city dog, he moves like a wolf. He wears dark boots tight up to the calves, drapes sand-silks over his mouth and neck. Besides his lizard eyes, only his hands are bare. He reveals a head of tangled black hair, dread-locks some of em. A beard patches up his face, thick but short. I notice weapons hanging from a belt: a rope, an ax, a couple of black blades. I gulp after counting em off. The blades are black, clean, well shined.

Shiv says mid-crunch, "Nah, we might leave him. Whattya think Key?"

The other man shrugs. His eyes are narrow-slitted and his face packed with dirt and maybe blood. A military khopesh hangs loose in his fingers. I don't say a word of it, but I figure I'm among outland mercenaries.

There is something unsettling about the air, the way it smells and tastes when shared with hardened killers. I try to smile but can't.

"Let him alone, Shiv," The Minister says, standing. "Won't leave a man to die. Have you learned one thing in this endless desert-plain?"

Shiv laughs bitter, but doesn't answer.

Nodding, I move to stand. I want me messages and to be gone. I get weight on me legs and the knee pops out loud. Pain spikes up me leg as I topple, and bite the sand. A croak escapes from me throat.

Shiv's giggling to himself. "Ack-quit yer groaning, pup. If you'd like, we'll make even on what happened here."

"Make even?" I cry out. "With what, I don't even know what the hell happened."

Shiv tosses me apple core into the dry wind and takes a few angry paces toward me. "I'll cut yer throat you little shit."

Between Shiv and me steps The Minister. He says, "Young pup. They would prefer you lay here to rot. You have no horse and one leg, and little option but death. Ah, but here is an option: decide daily to live, or not. Decide now." His voice settles into a whisper. "And know you have protection till your arrival in Crawing, as you mention." The Minister grins. His teeth look wooden. "The pack needs a guide of sorts. Will you work and call it even?"

Leaning forward, I nurse me knee, more to consider his little proposal than to help the pain. "Could ye tell me happened out here?" I got to know how me horse was killed. But I also want to know about the dangers of turning down they offer.

"Some fuckin prakas speared yer horse as you rounded the cliff-hold." Shiv points toward Nine-pay, a cave in big salmon colored walls where I hide out to eat me lunch on mother days. "You fell out the saddle, and they pinned you. Luckily, Key noticed the dust cloud and got his bow on em. Riddled a couple a those bastards."

I groan and lift up, me muscles tight. When I want to ask em what happened to the rest, I notice Key again and don't really want the answer. So I say, "How long's I out?"

Shiv spits. "Couldn't let you roast. Yer of use, pup. Drink up. Then show us to Crawing and maybe be on yer own way."

I think about it for a moment, not longer. "Where ye all moving in from?"

The Minister swats gnats from his face. "Will you guide the pack into town, maybe join for an ale there? Answer quickly."

Dust stirs up in me face as they move horses in me direction. The Minister's horse is pretty, its fur red with clouds of smoke furling into its feathery mane. He lets his lizard eyes fall upon me as I lie there. Fully aware I can die, I raise me hand to him.

He takes it, pulls me onto his horse's saddle. "Welcome," he says, looking to the road.

"Which way to Crawing?" The Minister's head turns first to the south, then to the north.

I point between the two and that fast his horse is on a gentle gallop. Shiv and a quiet man named Key are tight to our trail. Solus chases us through the desolate, scarred lands miles and miles outside glorious Sargafa.

I, a messenger, ride alongside three foreigners who I know to be enemy outlaws of Mirshan. As we gallop on toward Crawing, I give a quick thought to me home and family. I hope they're safe. A battle tore through town worse than a windstorm, I hear. Parts of that bother me, others don't. Having me land darkened with the shadow of southern battalions makes me fearful, but hungry. Messengers don't get paid well by the script but I'm used to peddling extras to those who want em. Many a coin out here in the Djad, I'm finding. Even for a mere boy like me.

Ha, me a pup? How many summers in the Solus-scorched landscape might a boy spend to be a man? Fifteen? If so, I might be more man than they.

Much less lucky, I figure. "We ought to ride through the night," I yell out. "Keep the horses warm that we might find a cool cavern for the daytime."

From behind, I note the rider's brief hint of a nod. He slows Redfur's pace to a trot, stroking her smokey mane. "The boy's true," he says. "Might you know of such a cavern, young pup?"

I say that I do.

"Point to the path," The Minister says quiet.

Toward a rocky-ridge ecru in the horizon, I raise me blistered hand. I had been in em ridges, which feels good to know. Might these men be lost without me, I might drag a job down after all. That too, feels pretty good.

We spend the cold night drifting swift across the blade-like expanse, like wind sweeping over a dune. Although it's a bumpy ride, I've been riding the Djad for a year or better. So it ain't that bad. I keep me hands warm by rubbing em together and blowing hot air over em and keeping em tight in me armpits. As we ride beneath a sky so vast it's oppressive, I sway me eyes from the riling clouds of desert scalp to the darling ebony sea above me. The way that sky is dotted with diamond-colored stars is beautiful.

So I wish to rest among em someday.

Through the night I hear Shiv talking to Key but not the other way around. Key's a really quiet man. Shiv goes on about skirmishes and his company and mentions me town. Says people there fled by the time any mercenaries arrived. I sigh. It's been less than a month since I saw me family but I still worry about em. They are a farming family and for whatever reason, me dad's opinion of the life is a low one, so here I go. Told me the last I seen of him to get moving. See and do better things. And if I hit hard times, he always got a shovel and fork for me at the shanty. Good man, me dad.

Badlands are full of bone Coyotes. I'm thankful as we go that The Minister's Redfur is quicker and fuller than any desert dog we chance to encounter. But I deceive ye not, those damn dogs are dangerous in packs. It's a fact.

Before dawn, the sky bruises, and turns purple and ugly and Solus like a pink eyeball rises and Aerth heats under its gaze. From the sands a wine-like fog is drawn. It's still cool when we approach the pale, broken ridges.

Redfur trots in a circle, leery.

"There something to be afraid of, pup?" Shiv asks.

I shake me head, but how the hell do I know? "Another camp, that's the worse of it. Crawing's a couple days out if ye cut the paths through the ridges. I know em."

The Minister reins Redfur to the base of a crack in the tanned walls and turns his head side-wise, saying, "Might she be fine here, young pup?"

I say yes and scope out the area best I can. "By twilight we'll be through this ridge. I don't reckon we rest all daylight." When no one answers, I tense up and feel pain in me leg. "But can if ye want."

Shiv laughs but I'm not sure at what. I glare at him quick. He's always got a grin. Key's attention is on his hands where he's rolling a cig. He feels me looking, methinks, and pokes his head up. Cold scorn chisels his features so I jolt me eyes away. Key raises me hair.

They unpack in the cavern. Indigo stone shavings from the cave's ceiling lay on the floor beside an old broken spit. Charred arbol dust outlines old footprints, ghosts of man past. I wipe em away quick, sure to not start a spook. Shiv swaggers to me with a wooden mug in his off-paw, a bottle of wet-ale in the other. "Yer a man today, pup." He chuckles, and pours me a pint and lets me to it.

By damn that shit hits hard, let me tell ye. And burns! I cough on it a bit and then laugh at meself. Shiv's laughing, too. The Minister unbundles a few jerky rations and sets em aside.

"Young pup, help find shade for the steeds," he says, heading out the cave.

Spittle drips out me mouth and then I follow him. I rub me eyes, trying to look at Shiv. "What the hell'd ye give me?"

He shakes his head and points out.

So there I go. The Minister treads across what look like untouched waves of caliche, Redfur and the other two near. They ain't tied, which is curious but I don't say anything. He's wordless and I'm tense.

"I'd bet it we hit a smaller cave round here," I say. "Might need a watch for em."

He nods. "Be out and about, will you, young pup?" The Minister's voice is friendly, methinks. It's got a welcoming-tone, like an innkeeper's. But ary time I hear em, I get chills.

I swallow. "If ye'd want me to, I'd watch over em."

The Minister nods again, lowering his sand-silk veil. His hair is tangled like willow branches. "Figure on having company," he says, taking swift sniffs at the air. "None wanted, either. Key'll keep watch."

"What makes him so tough?"

He laughs, too close to a sigh for me to miss it. "Key has seen the worst of war, young pup. No man should find wisdom he's found in so short of time."

"Not ye neither?"

"Recognizing wisdom within is like forming a friendship, isn't it? Once it's finally understood that two people are friends, they've most likely been for quite some time."

I nod. Me eyes tear up from dust gathering in em. "War's the way to wisdom," I say, raising me hand to shield me face.

"Ah." The Minister's lips curl in a grin. "For men like Key."

I shake me head.

"You're not too young to understand, are you?"

"I don't know."

He lets his eyes bore into mine. I try saying something, nothing forms, we end up in another cavern before I know it. We've been walking a while, though. Me leg's burning like a cig. I try not to limp all the way through the sun-stained cut in the ridge, but I can't really avoid it.

The Minister pets Redfur and whispers something into her ear. She huffs and does a playful stomp. "You should splint that." He admires that horse's beauty for a couple awkward moments. I just stand there, all but scratching me own ass. Then he walks toward me, past me, and stops at the mouth of the cave. I'm about to follow.

"They're smart enough to know where it's safe out here," he says to me, peering out. "Never lead them toward death and they trust humans better than lap dogs."

I think of Priea and feel a bit unnerved, a bit guilty. Lonely. Not sure if he knows it but that horse was close to me. Not sure if he knows, but before he came along, it was the Djad, Priea, and me. No creepy outlaw mercenaries. I huff aloud and he looks at me with those snake-eyes.

"Nothing was meant by it, young pup," says The Minister. He senses me blush. "This here's of a different breed of equine." There's a ghost. He wants to smile but doesn't. "A gift of God, mind you."

I really get confused and just let it drop. Redfur looks deep into me eyes. Hers are dark like lantern oil. Something about em are better than this world and that's the only way I'll explain it. It makes me smile and yet feel sad. Like that body of hers is a coffin for a living soul. I feel like I see it, a fleeting spark in her eyes.

Then we leave. Priea and Redfur are bad tastes in me mouth.

Our back trip is silent. He walks with long strides. I figure he treads more ground than it looks. The Minister's a deceiving man, methinks. He's got his secrets. But then again we all do.

When we come in Shiv is out cold, a pint of that hell-fire drink settled on his gut. Key's taking a stone to his khopesh, fining the edges with precise strikes. He knows what he's doing. Wise in the ways of war. I purse me lips and take a spot nearer to the cave's mouth and farther from any of those mercenaries. It's warmer here, which makes stone a bit cozier. It's not long till me eyes get heavy and sleep sets in just right.

*

What wakes a sleeping man? Nightmares, loud noises, and pain. I'm awake to all of these. Sweat is thick on me hairline, I'm so goddamned hot. Hot as a bull. I can't really see, but I know I'm alone and I panic. Me throat's dry and all I'm thinking is that I ain't got no water if those mercs've left me. Realize now that I'm bound to die a long one without em.

Good God. It takes some amount of fortitude to shake that off. But when I jump up, me knee cracks like a twig and I'm hopping in circles. Outside there's clatter, metal clanging and I try to rush toward it, but me leg doesn't hold me weight the way it should. But limping like all hell, into the red day I come. Down the ridge I stop at a bluff and look over. Rain-colored funnels of dust are tumbling with the shadows of men whirling violent inside em. I hustle back in the cavern, me eyes peeled for any kind of weapon.

Key's bow's out, arrows and all spilled around the fire spit, telling me the pack's caught on they heels. I gather the bow and those arrows in me arms, and drag me leg out the cavern.

It's hot and the sweat in no way helps me vision. The noise of they tussle is growing more desperate. I can feel it. As quick as me hands can manage I nock an arrow. A bunch of dark men, Sargafans, got the pack surrounded. The dust settles around the outlanders. It looks lke six on two. Key and Shiv. It's six on three when me arrow's loosed.

It flies pretty. A dark man falls, the others reeling with they eyes to the caves. To me. I duck out of the way, me hands trembling mad as hell. I can't get another arrow nocked before I feel sick in me gut. Em goddamn Sargafans are down in the hardpan shouting war-commands and cuss words from the bottoms of they lungs. I peek out, huffing like a horse. Two Sargafans have disappeared, but methinks they ain't dead.

They're probably looking for me.

I limp low into an alcove the size of a cartwheel and tuck me knees hard into me chest. I try me best to settle me lungs, counting in me head 1, 2. 1, 2…

A shadow forms over the trail, homing in as if tracking me scent. That shadow crawls in the heat of the Djad. Me legs are trembling. Goddamn, I killed one of em.

It's closer. I can hardly hear the steps but I got nothing else to hear except me heart beating and those steps. Me throat dries like dust.

The shadow stops.

"Come out, young pup." It's the voice of The Minister.

I almost cry, climbing out the alcove. He's there long and gaunt and towering over. His sand-silks are spotted with blood.

I hobble past him and look to the hardpan field. Key's got a man under his arm. The slick khopesh tears open the Sargafan's throat. I look away so fast I don't see the blood run out. But it's too quiet: I hear it splash.

Shiv's laughter fills the ridge, echoing like a nightmare. Me back's against the ecru rock wall when I sit me ass the whole way down.

Shiv looks at me hard in the eye. "Good shooting," he says. "Yer even with me, pup."

I nod and close me eyes, and pass out. This is one kind of a welcome to the Djad.

*

Are ye kidding me? They prod me awake quick as owl shit. The Minister has me leg wrapped, two arbol branches set straight in a splint. He's pissed off. "You didn't listen, young pup." Me knee's throbbing like a toothache. Shiv's chewing up jerky while wiping away our signs of encampment. I don't see Key anywhere but he's got to be around. "Should the pack leave here?" The Minister shows his teeth. They are dirty and gnarled enough to be wooden.

I nod and lift me hide up to me good leg. "God-damn. Me leg ain't festering, is it?"

He shakes his head and looks away. He listens to the wind. "Lead the pack out of here, young pup. Toward the town of Crawing."

"No choice, zaer. Me horse's dead. I got me message and I should deliver it. More that it's you who's helping me."

"They got water in Crawing?" Shiv asks. His voice is serious. "We might get in at night and wash up. Whattya think?"

I nod. "They got two wells," I tell em. "Center village. Aryone uses it but they got one behind the inn, too. Use that for public baths and whatnot. I could get us a room there. I'm in oft enough. Message business, ye see."

The Minister whistles, breathy and quiet. The wind blows all round us and for a minute I blame it on him. Redfur and the other two babes come trotting out the cave. I stand still, in awe of em. Shiv throws his chessack over his shoulder and mounts his steed.

"Key's cleaning up the base of the ridge." The Minister says. "Take this horse down to him. Meet on the east road to Crawing." He helps me mount Key's horse, a camel-furred beast with a midnight mane. "She moves swift as any you'll ride, young pup. Careful now." Then he kicks her in the ass and we're off.

She rides like Priea. And if I hadn't been riding the region for so long a time, I'd be eating dirt by now. We hustle down white-hot slopes, ducking rocky overpasses that look like spider webs above our heads. We gallop off the path to the other side of the ridge, where the rock's more pink than tan.

Near a wide crevice in the pink rock, flies and gnats and other shit gather like a sandstorm. I slow the horse down and tumble off, probably a bit too curious. Scared of me knee cracking, I hit the dirt in a push-up. Key's horse trots a few feet away and settles down nice and easy in the heat.

So now what the hell do we have here? I'm crawling toward the little hole, an insect buzz budding like an incoming squall. Solus heats the back of me neck and shoulders. Cold sweat runnels through the knots of me spine.

There are blood driblets on the edge of the opening, brown and dry. The golden hardpan below is carved by scarlet claw-runs. I shuffle backward, frightened. Me heart picks up. Key's horse neighs and spins a circle. I look at her quick and then back to the crevice.

Holding me breath I reach in there, into the darkness of that grotto, and feel around. The rock's cool to the touch. Wiggling me fingers, I can feel insects swarming upon me hand and arm. They raise me hairs but I keep reaching. Something like cold moss masses between me fingers. I get a fistful and reel back like I'm saving me mum from drowning. It's got a bit of weight to it, like a sack of onyx stones. Dust gathers under me eyes and in me brow and nose. I fight it through the wound and swipe the dust away and let it settle. In me hands is the head of a rotting Sargafan, sun-browned to the bone. His hair's tangled in me fingers and I scramble to get it out. His throat was opened before the full decapitation. The tang of wet-forged iron pinches me nostrils.

I stand and hobble in a circle spitting, squinting toward Key's horse. Tears clog up me eyes with dirt and gnats. I sit back down.

He was young, but still older than me. Seventeen? He was still proud of his moustaches. Sargafans are always lean, especially the prakas, and they line they lips with moustaches. I want to kick him so goddamn bad. His kin killed me horse, fucked with me mission. I ought to cut your throat again, ye bastard. Unkind words and trails of spit are flying from me mouth at this point. Can hardly keep control of meself.

Then I see the Sargafan's stomach: Where a man's mom-scar should be, about the center of a belly, there is a black hole backed up with blood. It's a wound thick enough for me to fist. Me head jerks away and most immediate I blast yellow bile into the dirt.

Key prowls around the shade side of the ridge, that curved, bloody tool a shadowy extension of his arm. I give a swift whistle, wiping off me mouth.

Key aims his narrow gaze toward me and his horse, and rushes low in me direction, khopesh slung at his side. He helps me on his horse without a word about me yellowed-clothing or about the desecrated Sargafan. I manage to tell him we're meeting on the east side of the ridge. He whips the reins and his girl's hard on a gallop, quiet as the moon.

We meet up on the east road. The Minister and Shiv might have been ten minutes ahead at a slow pace. The hot sun must have shone its zenith in me sleep and began to wander over the horizon by the time our horses hit the middle of the Djad. I slip between sleep and not sleep. How eyelids, so delicate and small, could become so heavy I can't understand, and can't hope to explain either. Seeing the Djad too long of a time is a burden no human can bear. When I pray, I pray that the burden will be easy— or that I make it so, or that it becomes so, or that I realize it so.

I smile and keep me head up-turned. Peer to the flesh-colored sky of a blossoming half-night. I feel something up there that I can't quite see down here. It may be nothing more than the source of light.

Aye. Nighttime will come, and with bitter quickness.

Solus doth abandon us.

And the skyline bleeds in a way that reminds me of a slit throat. So much that I get sick in me stomach and heave broadside from Key's horse. He pretends not to notice, and that's fine.

I know the way to Crawing. But there are small places that are closer and I mention it to em.

The Minister asks me, "Which route would you take?"

I want to say the one back home. "Into Law-qen. Same way as Crawing, but a little west and closer to here," I tell em. "I get me food for the week there. A good bath, if ye be interested. They ask fewer questions in there. Less hunters."

"How's the ale?" Shiv says, patting me back.

I nod. "Suppose it's good. It works."

He grins, looks to The Minister. He's solemn as a cemetery. They meet eyes and The Minister shrugs.

"You say hunters, young pup... ...do you mean bounty hunters?"

"They run in numbers past Law-qen," I tell em. "Pretty dumb fellows, most of em. Law-qen's full of cowards." Aryone of these men's staring at me hard. "Out here they chance to be pretty tough."

Shiv snorts, jolts his steed. "Then I believe we're fine, gentlemen."

The Minister gives me a weird eye that sends chills through me body.

"Closer we get to Sargafa, by now, more hunters out and at it. Looking for skirmish loot and worse. A lawless bunch of idiots, though," I say.

"Does Law-qen skirt most travel, young pup?" asks The Minister. His beady eyes stake a place in me own.

"Mostly. That's a reason I take to it. Less of em to hassle me about me job. It's the farthest from Sargafa and Crawing's simply bigger. More rooms, more ale. More arything."

The Minister pulls his reins in deep and turns Redfur about. "You will lead, young pup. Suggest you make haste before the worst of the night seeps in."

I smile weak. It's going to get cold. "Indeed," I whisper. "It's a few hour ride. Still. Better than a couple of days ride."

Shiv and Key face each other but say nothing. I can only see Shiv's face and he doesn't look happy. He's suspicious of me, methinks. That's just like him, though. He says to me, "Why'd you leave it out before, pup? Before? Why'd you leave it out?"

I shrug. "I'm already late."

"How bout that," he says back to me.

I squint and look away from him.

"You ain't too young to fib." He grits his teeth. "Know what I mean, don't you?" The Minister just watches, his lips pressed in a stern line. "Why, pup?" Shiv asks. "Why'd you leave it out?"

"Hell I didn't know it mattered."

"Well, well. Hear this shit?"

"Forget it." The Minister raises one hand. "Upon arrival at Law-qen, young pup, you will compose a map of the region in accordance with your fullest knowledge. No one." He pauses to spit. "No one will harm you if you remain true. Understand?"

I swallow. "But I ain't no artist."

"Do you think the pack needs a portrait of the queen?" His eyes are wide and focused. "Your best will suffice."

"Then we call it quits with one another. Take no offense, Minister. But I got me own shit to take care."

He nods. "Sure. Be even then, young pup. From there, God knows. Do what you must to survive." Those words hit me like cold water.

*

Law-qen is a small town, possessed of clay or light wooden shanties and deer hide tents used by nomadic peoples from further west. Wanderers of the wild come in and trade they hides and meats for buckets of well water and tools. Mostly they're peaceful next to prakas, but I hear they got territories to protect, too. That they do so with they hearts before em in a way it should be done.

We ride close to town at dawn. The light is cold and brassy. Wind tussles arbol, clots of tumbleweed arcing wicked over the hardpan as if escaping unseen, unspeakable terrors.

The world is fast asleep, breathing steady and quiet against the clop of hooves. Smoke from furnace chimneys clump in a cloud looming over Law-qen like a temple bell. Women are waking, emerging from abodes as ants with gray clothing in they claws. I smell eggs distant as a whistle wafting on the wind. Hog slices and fresh game. Law-qen wakes with the caws. It ain't long till the hammers of industry are clunking atop a gurgling resurgence of folk who're alive after life.

We come in with blinking awe, a stand still worthy of a swashbuckling street-duel. Silence follows us to the stable where The Minister ties Redfur and the others. It's mere moments I push Fancy's door open. A bar, brothel, and restaurant. Seediest hut I ever saw meself but they pemmican's delicious and so is other stuff, I hear.

Brap is the barman and owner of Fancy. An old fighter for Mirshan, he's now only old. Has scars up his wooden head to scare outcasts from messing with em. He's fought in The War, they say. Some war long passed now. . .about which me dad cares to keep secret. But Brap survived and thrives on the stale bounties of emptied battlefields, methinks. His mustache is like moonlight against his midnight skin. He scans the three outlanders from behind the bar. He's got a grin that's worn ary time I meet him.

"What need ye, Mousai?" he asks, not looking at me. "A room for road-weary travelers?"

I nod. "Might it that ye fix me a room, Brap and I'll sweep up in here. And scrub out the mugs for ye."

"Fixed for coppers, I reason." He presses his lips together. "Aye, but yer honest folk. If ye tired, best get to restin. Yer no good to me weak, boy." Brap clasps his hands and blows in em.

"Cold morning," I say.

He laughs and leads us through a dingy hall to the room where light peels the dark corners through an antelope door. The Minister looks me over quick and then settles himself in. Shiv stares out the window for as long as I know while Key pats his khopesh for a painful five minutes before fatigue rips through me like nervous current and I'm out.

*

A couple of hours pass when Brap comes for me. He raps loud enough me eyes bulge open. Methinks The Minister is staring out the window when I wake but it's quite hard to say. His lizard eyes are hidden behind a waterfall of tangled black hair so Hell, he might be looking at me. His ax ain't slung, either. It's set atop the sill in height apt enough for swift armament.

"I'll be out," I call, sounding like I caught a fly.

"All right, son. I need ye to straighten up my bar. Gonna run across town and talk to Blacksmith Jim fore he leaves. Ye look after Fancy."

I yell, "Alright Brap," and gather up me bones. To the pack I say,

"I allow you'll all want some whiskey or something later. Be on me, since I'm—"

"That's fine, young pup." The Minister sneers. His eyes are yet pointed outside.

I pull me boots tight and roll me sleeves back. "I'll get me some hide and ink, draw ye a map of the Djad. Surprised ye haven't one before now."

"That surprises you?"

"Ye ain't from too far away, now are ye?"

"There are no maps for places like this." His lips part in a smile that vanishes quick like a snuffed candle. "Young pup. Do not leave your employer waiting."

I nod to him and head to the bar. Fancy's a cavern for traders who've gone the wrong way, and for outlaws who need food before heading into the desert to hide again. I like it here because me dad and Brap go back to fighting days. Through him, I get free passage for the most part. People here don't mess with me lest they provoke the lion in Brap. And he ain't no comical beast, let me say. Once chucked a thug across the bar and sliced his face up because he badmouthed one of the girls.

Well, I reason not to ruin something good while I'm here.

Only a few people are sitting in the tavern. They're huddled at a table playing roq-cha. The tick clicking of bone dice sets rhythm to me work. I grin and take up the broom and fill they mugs with frothy warm beer when they are low. One of em rolls up a cig for me and lights it right quick. Snatch and snap. He snickers. I hear embers crackling, heavier when me lungs pull for em. The smoke's itchy and hot, but it soothes me nerves by the time it's burnt out and I'm sweeping again.

I say thanks to the man and he nods. I ask, "Who's up in coin here?"

"Reckon I am, Mousai," another man says to me, raking in a small pot. He's paler than most around here with unshaven whiskers and eyes set wide on his head like a fish or something. A tan flop hat shades much of his face. But methinks a hating eye gleams through most anything. I don't trust him.

"Have we met, zaer?" I ask, hardly sure.

He shakes his head. "I've seen ye. Crawing and such. A young man, a messenger," he says to his friends, not me. "Really wondering if ye'd ever show here."

"Well, why's that? I'm in here oft enough." I stop sweeping entirely.

"I reckon you ain't got good reason to know a man like me," he says. The man tosses the dice and then tips his hat. "Name's Sal, warden of the Djad. Eleventh lieutenant to Raija Saryone years ago." This is when I notice the lines of his face, deep like dried rivers. "Ye likely ain't know me by anything but zaer. A beaten word, I reason."

He is right about both things. "Well."

"Well." Sal laughs, shaking his head.

It's quiet a while, the kind of quiet when aryone thinks what they're going to say but no one's talking. "I got work– "

"Right. I'll need ye ear, then. A little later, aye?" He pulls a small pot and winks at me.

"I'll be riding out this eve, Sal. Having me a drink and riding to Crawing."

"That's what I need ye for. But don't be impatient, son. I got a good tale for ye." Sal sniffs like a goddamn Coyote hunting dead. But he's the one who stinks.

I hobble out the main lounge and wind through the hall back to me room. Drawing heavy breaths with each stiff move. But I don't go the whole way. I don't show em I'm afraid. Instead I wait for me lungs to calm, walk out proud as I can, and keep sweeping.

Though I feel em staring at me from time to time, I ignore it best I can. It ain't long till Brap comes back, chessacks full a tinker-tools and some cocoa. He settles in swift, counts they coin and asks me what I gave out and I tell him not much. I then nod toward a back room and harden me eyes. He's snappy in the know and takes lead.

When we're out of view, I whisper: "Who is that man? The one with the hat. A soldier, Brap?"

"He used to be a soldier, aye. When Saryone was Emperor. A damn fine one. Sal, he's called. A name heavy on the purse if ye work in Sargafa."

I give him a confused look.

"I reason he's a hunter, Mousai. But he ain't in here oft as you. Much less in point a fact."

"How ye know of him, then?" I ask, a bit louder than desired. I can almost feel they devilish ears perk.

"Oh by God, son. Trust me," he says with a grin. "And I tell ye another thing. I don't call it dumb luck he's here now." This he punctuates with a stern glance and a palmed gold coin, the likes of which I ain't seen before. "Ain't Mirshanni. I know that," he says.

"Hell does that mean? What's he here for, Brap?"

He doesn't answer, just shakes his head. "I don't know." Then he goes to leave and I step in front of him.

"Brap, is it something with me? The hell've I done?"

"Ah, God be damned, Mousai. Have ye looked at the company ye keep? They're a band a dogs, ye ought know it by now. They ain't from here, and they ain't yer brothers neither. However ye found em, that's yer business. But I allow you rid of em."

"It pisses me off, Brap. Who are they? I can't have men around I can't trust. Look after me till Crawing? I can't do that. It's only been yer help and me family up till they saved me from the Djad— from goddamned prakas."

"I don't know, son. They a dangerous folk to hang about. Especially with other dangerous folk hunting em."

I shake me head, knowing how he's right but that I can't tell em more. "I got to make even on something. After that. Who knows, I drift off. Go back to me ways. Maybe even farm rice or beans with me dad. But they saved me. I owe em that."

He looks away and cracks his knuckles. "Ye get yer hide outta this fast as possible, Mousai. I ain't keen on letting any damn person hurt ye."

"Ye better be including those thugs out there."

He laughs hearty like a twilight fireplace. "So be it, son."

I sigh. And it takes me a few to reclaim calm but I do it and then we back out in the bar. Brap sneaks in a stern glance possessed of eyes of an ancient bear. I take up cleaning again while Brap tinkers with cooking hot cocoa. I tell him, "I ain't had it before. But I'll try some."

He grins, darting his eyes to me, and away real quick. "Well, it ain't no grain ale, Mousai," he says. "But it tastes awful good. Got it from Blacksmith Jim. Says it comes from the Free Lands west of here."

I nod. "Ain't been out there, neither."

All the while Sal's burning holes in me skin. I can't stare back. He's scary in a Shiv-like-too-happy-to-do-me-job kind of way. He's one of em out there who's paid for the heads of anyone against the Mirshan empire.

A couple of women push open the door, scanty hides hanging loose over they shoulders. "A round, Brap," one says. She is pretty by me reason, thin with cute bones and whorl lashes.

"Don't be blushing, boy," Sal jeers. His idiot friends snort, laugh. Poke elbows.

"I ain't," I say. "What I got to do with em anyway?"

"Not a damn thing," Sal says. He tosses the dice away and his eyes jump and center on me. "Be here in an hour, Mousai. Got business, you and I. But that's then," he says. "Now, I got other business."

Lady tells em all, "We ain't whorin tonight so get yer goddamn cunny elsewhere." Brap tightens up. I see it.

And Sal too is red in the face. "Sure, now?" he reaches in his pouch. "I got gold in here," he says, beckoning her closer. We all stop moving, as if at theater. The Lady takes a couple of steps and that quick Sal lunges and puts a damn blade at her naked neck.

I shout at him nothing memorable.

He doesn't look at me. "Aye, ye are lucky, whore. If they weren't young folk present I'd make a new mouth of yer throat."

I swallow hard. "Cut her, ye bastard. And ye'll have to cut up this entire bar. I reason ye ain't got no goddamned back up except these blow-hards."

"Mousai."

"Now ye got an option or two, old timer," I say. Me fingers are yellow, tight around the broom handle.

Sal laughs from the back of his throat. "Ye ready to have a dead whore on yer mind, boy?"

"Ain't me mind ye'll be hurting, zaer," I tell him.

"Mousai. Maybe that's enough."

"Ain't mine, either." Sal looks at me now. He's grinning, half his face lost beneath his hat. "Not one of ye have half a wit to stop me from any damn thing. So I'm a take her to a backroom and ye know what I intend? I'm a fuck'er bloody. And leave my seed. That shit's as good as gold." He grabs her by the hair, reels it around a tight fist. She groans and looks at all us with antelope eyes.

"Brap, this ain't right."

He stands in a quiet paralysis, his knees near-buckled. I want to club him and ary one in the tavern.

Sal shoves her hard into a near wall and leads her across the bar. I choke up in tears and heft the broom. Ain't no one going to do a thing? No? I'll wail that bastard.

"I wouldn't move," a man says from behind me. "I'll stick ye between the ribs."

I hear a whoosh. The slice of air. Out of instinct I drop to the floor. Blood splatters and the table crashes, splaying splinters of wood. I duck under me hands and look around.

Rooted in that man's skull stands an ax. Its wooden handle thin and vibrating.

Before I get up, Sal's piling through a far window. The Minister hurls himself past me in an arcing blur. He's silent as he moves.

Again, I become a watcher. A speck of dust on the wall. The Minister hacks down the other in seconds and Sal escapes to the outside. Dirt kicks up behind him. Me heart sinks low when I see he's already on his horse.

I wanted him dead.

"Who are they, young pup?" say The Minister. His hands are planted around the sill. Black locks of hair branch out chaotic. "Who are they?" He growls.

"H-hunters. By God. Hunters, Minister."

"And perchance, might you know whom they're hunting?"

I swallow. "I know now."

He nods but doesn't look at me. Brap's bringing his girls out the bar. I'm boiling over him but don't say anything. The whores do. They complain. But I can't listen to em it hurts so bad.

"A map, young pup. You don't have too long to draw it."

I look down, and kick some dirt.

"Victory is not always killing the enemy." I ain't sure what he means by that. The Minister moves past me. He gets his ax from the guy's skull, as it lies split and gray on the floor. Sounds briefly like when ye gut a deer. He finally looks at me and gets close. His lizard eyes are black, and big. He grabs me arm and I recoil at his chilly touch. But he's weirdly gentle. He reaches for me hair and stops breathing.

Then he just goes back to the room, silent like a breeze.

"The fuck's into all of ye?" I say to no one. I lift Sal's mug of whiskey and down a throat-full, and then another.

The room is empty and I am alone. There is blood on the floor four inches from me feet. "And what the hell wrong's with you, Brap?"

I fall to me ass exhausted and crawl beneath another table. Me nerves are like hot snakes trembling in the hell of me body, and I try to calm em. But I can't. Within me a heart beats hard like drums of war, and I can't calm down.

*

Half-drunk I get a quill and some hide and start scribbling up what I know of the region. Hopefully it'll come out okay, but at this point I don't give a fuck really. So triangles for the Hydra Sigh mountains, west; dots for Crawing, Law-qen, and Quriah, which is east, towards the great River of Sleep and its canyons; a broken line to separate the oasis from the desert; a solid line for the many roads, one of the river well east. I draw up places I've found interesting, like Nine-pay. If I remember something specific about a place, I throw it on there. On the side, I etch notes the best I can, but me hand-writing is awful scratchy and I reckon the words ain't too sensible.

Shiv and Key walk past me. Both are armed to the teeth. Out Fancy they skulk, not a word or a glance to be stolen from em. Brap and a younger lady are talking business in the corner of the bar. I'm still pissed at him. More than I've been at anyone, methinks. Till today, a part of me considered him family.

Me face burns hot and I decide to stop thinking about him simply because it might get me in trouble to do what I feel like. With the map rested in me hands I limp back to me room, hoping The Minister will deem it worthy. I nudge open the door with me good knee.

Good God, what is this—some sign of gratitude?

The Minister presses a naked girl against his body. She's face-first against a wall. The Lady. Her moan is blissful and I think genuine. I stare too long and she notices. He doesn't seem to. I close the door, put me back against the wall, limp down the hall then out of Fancy. Outside I piss on the wall and sing a song and then decide it's best I get back in.

At the fireplace I hold the map up so the ink dries. The fire there keeps me warm too. When nights hit in the Djad, it's always a harsh feeling– like waking up to someone pulling the covers off. For a few moments, I stir up the ash and think of where to get arbol for later– if we were to stay.

*

How old are you? Fifteen, sixteen? A girl whispers, calm and confident.

"Aye." She is beautiful. Her hair is like silver threads. Her face is pale, her eyes gray.

Isn't that a bit young to travel alone? This place must be scary. Her accent is foreign but I understand her.

I look at her again. "I ain't alone."

Brap's silhouette disappears into a vacant room. I hear him muttering to himself with the swipe of broom bristles hushing him only a slight.

"Aye. The land's scarier than the people."

She hides a smile, but not well. I meant that, anyway. I thought my father and I might starve it's so dry here. We didn't, of course.

"Well," I say, pulling on me shirt. "Long way from

home, then."

Yes. She nods. My father doesn't like Brap. So I do the most of the talking for him. "Anyway," I tell her. "I'm Mousai, I deliver messages."

Her eyes are solid and stone-colored; they focus on me hard. I'm Wrayth. She reaches out with one hand and I just look at her.

She grabs me at the forearm and wraps me fingers around hers.

"In the Djad, we don't touch," I say.

I watch her as she watches the rest of the room, but then Shiv barges inside, screaming. "Get the hell out of here! Minister! Let's go! We got company! Thirty strong, maybe a couple minutes ride."

In his wake, chairs are tossed along with wooden mugs and clay pots. It sounds like the sky is falling.

Before I stand, she comes close to me and says, The universe, Mousai, has collapsed around you and me.

I stare at her, blinking but once, and swallow.

You and your men follow me; I know of a place.

"Where?" I cry, hobbling toward the door.

It's a church. It's old and abandoned but we haven't been visited there yet. Not by bandits or hunters. Or knights, for that matter.

I nod. "Shiv!"

His stare is a sharp knife. "What you want, you shit?"

I'm quiet for too long.

"You deaf, pup?"

"No."

Wrayth stands up. There's a church toward the western mountains, she says.

"There's a church near. It's perfect, Shiv. Sal thinks we're headed to Crawing tonight, if anywhere."

The Minister steps out of the darkness. His vision darts to Shiv.

"If it works, fine. If we get caught up, pup, I'm leaving yer carcass behind me."

"Ain't me they looking for, though." I say, walking out. "Let's go. Ain't none of us here want to get caught up, Shiv."

"The boy is true," The Minister says, hefting an ax. "Young pup."

"Aye?"

"Bring round the horses. If they are closing in now, there isn't much time."

Before he finishes, Wrayth and I are in the streets of Law-qen. We round em up and it seems Redfur knows what's happening. She prances, more anxious than ever. The stable smells of shit and dead earth and we hustle through hard-packed earth to get em out. Wrayth unsheathes a flat knife from her hip and tears the tethers.

You have a horse in here? She asks.

I say no and lead our three out.

Here, she says. Take this one. She cuts the tether to a pale horse and quickly leads us out. Now come on.

We ride passed Fancy. The Minister crouches at the corner and we all watch with him as little bulbs of light flicker over a sand dune maybe a couple minutes out of town. I count fifteen on me own.

"Let's go," I say to em and Wrayth climbs atop the horse with me. The Minister's look is hard but he listens without a word. "Lady says get out to the west. By morning we ought arrive?" I ask.

She nods.

Key and Shiv appear from behind a clay hut, both at arms. Shiv says to me, "Well, pup. You better fix this one or else yer in for a slow one."

"A slow what?" I say, as if to challenge him. "Ye ain't got reason not to trust me. Sal could a had ye bright and early if I allowed. But it ain't like that, Shiv. I owe ye all. Follow me out. It ain't gonna be too much but it's either that or ye outrun scores of hunters. Up to you." I rattle the reins beneath me horse.

He stares and then spits. His nod is barely visible. "Then we should hurry," he says and starts his horse behind the shacks rendering us invisible to the invaders.

The Minister whispers something to Key as they horses pass. The hiss of his voice raises hairs.

After we ride past all Law-qen's homes, it's like a jailbreak. I kick me horse and it sprints with its head low. Like a heartbeat, the hooves slog. We can see Sal's men rushing into town with orange torches hot and ready to burst em-selves upon Fancy and flesh. We ride faster and the heartbeat quickens, too.

Faster, faster until we ride upon a small encampment. Five black men, parkas or maybe mercenaries hop to they feet.

"A contingent?" says Shiv, and The Minister nods and narrows his lizard-eyes.

Five men, black as night, raise alarm. They heads pop up like spearheads. Key springs his bow into aim and fires a shaft with divine accuracy. The stone tip splits a Sargafan's nose and tears through the back of his skull, stuck. The others fumble for swords and javelins and spears and try to set against our charge. Shiv's horse is stabbed at the rib and propped upward. She bucks and huffs loudly, dancing in circles as if her hooves were set ablaze. Shiv rolls off, bringing a dagger into his grip.

"C'mon now," he says, licking his lips.

We on the horses circle around, and Wrayth's got one hand around me waist and a knife in her other. Shiv is flanked by two men with spears; they jab relentlessly yet he keeps em back. Key unleashes another arrow through one of they necks. I swallow and look away. Quickly, I reel me horse around and The Minister follows but not Key. He kicks his horse into a full charge and she leaps over the set spears; atop the saddle, he twists around, pulls a shaft tight, and lets it loose.

"Go on, Minister," he says, the first words I ever hear him say. "We have this under control. The bodies good as gone," he whispers as Shiv takes a man down.

"Hear, young pup? Lead!"

We ride on but I don't feel the warmth of Wrayth's breath at the back of me neck. When I face her, her eyes are wide and full of horror. Her chin quivers and tears mist in her glass-blue eyes. I watch em fall.

"Take your meat and leave," The Minister says, his eyes darting between Law-qen, me, and the vast gray desert before us.

It's often hard to ignore him but I do. I follow her line of sight and fall into a void of inescapable terror meself: in the violent shade of night, Key stands a silhouette like a demon torturing a soul in hell. He plunges a blade deep. We ride and ride and the screams last for full minutes and I wonder if those two will get us caught.

*

A man's life ain't the same after he's ended another's life. It's worse when he witnesses it and realizes he ain't keen on the horror to begin with. I can't tell ye what that moment did to me. I can't. And seeing the horror in Wrayth's eyes had kindled some kind of sensitivity within meself. I can't tell ye the all of it.

I watched those men, rode with em.

*

Half-light becomes nighttime with a jaw-locking chill. The moon as a soft watcher watches us with reluctant vision as we flick across the Djad, our bodies aching and our minds sore. A haze thick as butter blankets the horizon in yellow gauze as though Aerth is repairing her own wounds and the stars are acolytes of the healing clergy watching. Deeper down, I think of me heartbeat and I think of the clop of hooves and the sounds of fighting and the groans of suffering and I believe that nothing divine has ever protected its people and shouldn't either. I look at The Minister and wonder what god he follows, if any, and wonder if he is blessed by that god or if he The Minister blesses his brothers and wonder if maybe each deserves his victory, and therefore also his defeat.

Key and Shiv ride up, each on they horses. A dry red pervades all exposed skin and only the darkness of they clothes hides the blood on em. I can barely speak.

I choke up on dust, me mouth is so wide ope. "How is ye horse, Shiv?" I ask.

He grins as we ride but doesn't answer.

"Fine, then. Keep ye secrets," I say but am stunned into silence thereafter. I keep me eyes to the desert as we ride like drift-wood over the sea of caliche waves.

The wind blows against us but we ride harder. We move through black outlines of villages, emptied of humanity, though I feel the raking of farmers in the dead fields with they ploughs scraping away the calloused skin of the Djad and I hear the many children playing in the sparse shade of the orchards and the mother frying eggs for all except us riders who ride endlessly on an endless sea of sand.

Hours and hours pass but we see the dim glowing like rain-colored pearls high as if atop a mountain.

Wrayth pulls me tight and says, That's the church, dear man. Father's lit a small beacon for us.

I sigh and whip the reins, ready to rest.

*

To us the church is a fortress.

To the world, it's a forgotten haven for forgotten men.

The hollow mouth of the ridge forks out and the proud building stands well-guarded within, while the tower reaches high as though raping the night sky. A broken bell sways in the wind but is soundless and dry. Shiv hums nervous.

Blacksmith Jim is stationed here with well-hidden sentries posted atop stoneform parapets and I'm not certain why they don't attack. Why is he here?

She tells me not to worry but that ain't reassuring.

Blacksmith Jim, a figure as gaunt as the hungriest man in the Djad, slinks out the church, a dull glowing lamp hanging off his arm. "Who do we have?" The glare couldn't hide his leeriness. "Soldiers?"

Wrayth climbs off the horse, delicate in her step. Men in need. They were being hunted but, she says, looking sad, there is no current pursuit. She glances at Key.

He wipes his mouth and says nothing.

"Well come in, be quick," the man says and stifles the light, disappears into the haven for forgotten men.

I see very few things through the pallid light. Deep in the corners, there are men with jagged teeth and sunken eyes staring feverishly at us newcomers.

Jim himself wanders among em, a shade behind the golden glow of his lantern. He whispers and they hunger wanes.

"Were you followed?" Blacksmith Jim says.

She sets her chessack beneath a bed and turns to him.

"No," says Shiv grinning. "...Prakas prey on the outskirts of town. They've no reason to suspect you, zaer."

"And who might they be?" he asks, stepping closer.

"Sal's what he goes by," I say, looking to the floor. "A hunter."

Blacksmith Jim strokes his ratty white beard, stretching it out from his chin like a stocking. "Settle in. There are unused cots all over," he says without regarding me words. "You are in no immediate danger here."

I take me few things and push em underneath a cot and look around. The church is old and dusty but it ain't decrepit. A quaint smell like ancient tomes is thick in the dry air. In me short scope, I find no altars and any benches that may have been used long ago are missing. Instead, mud bricks pack a vacant floor. Weapons and cargo lay across it like altars they own-selves.

The Minister hasn't moved from the doorframe. He watches with his hand not far from the handle of his ax. The line of sight from his snake-like eyes climbs the walls and through the cracks of the walls and up the bell tower and through the sunken eyes of our company and through the souls of our company and he judges us.

Wrayth is seated not so far away, quietly pulling her boots off and massaging her calves. Her fingers are slender but seem to work hard. Blacksmith Jim walks close to her and whispers, "That happens again and I'll disembowel you."

She looks up at him and smiles. She then looks at me. Dear man. There's a bath outside. I reason you'd like one.

I startle and then kinda laugh. "Certainly, I would like a bath. Ye got a fire cooking around here?"

Jim lifts his eyes to me. "We do. But that isn't necessary. The water in the Djad is always warm —is it not?"

A man thin as a toothpick kicks open a door on the far side. I try to hide me limp across the floor and hear nothing but me own footsteps and it's like no one else is breathing but me. All of em seem to have died and are now decaying.

But it's fresh outside. Surrounding me is a fort-like fence almost like a hog pen with a water pump and in the bucket is a wiry brush and powder soap. It takes me full minutes to get any water flowing, but I do, and fill the bucket with water. I hang me clothes over the fence and look to the sky. It's clearer than I ever remember. Each star shines, vibrates, and calls to us, even those caught in the chalky light of Lunus; the smallest of stars remain significant.

I pour the water from the bucket over me and scrape the wire across the soap and across me body and keep me head down. I think of nothing except me family and wonder how they are and how they farm is. Knowing em, probably well. Taught me when I was even younger: this is the way things are done, Mousai. Get what ye put in and help another in need, and bless em all.

One more fill of the bucket and I let the warm water loosen me muscles. I move me hair from me eyes and then sigh, look up, put me clothes on, and walk back inside half-naked.

Flames make our shadows dance. Ten of us are in a circle. The Minister and his pack on one side with Blacksmith Jim and his men on the other. They keep contained to each other, remote and quiet. Each of em has a foreign leather about they shoulders and mechanic bows to they sides. Sharp swords are slightly out of the scabbards but more than fear em, I feel protected. Key and Shiv are rolling cigs, enough for all of us. Wrayth and I sit close to the middle and she is quiet. Methinks her eyes are forcibly softer here, but they nonetheless dance like the flames.

Blacksmith Jim eyes me suspicious and I can't help it but smile. He offers us food and we all take it with cheer. Whiskey and mulled wine, too. We drink and laugh, tell stories and fib a lot. Wrayth says nothing, but we laugh at her anyway and drink until the fire is low. We feed it arbol and kindling I ain't seen too much of before but when it smolders it smells like holidays at home.

Jim tells us about the forest the wood is from and tells us about the spooky goings-on: myths of the dying centaurs and rising dead; myths of traveling monks, conquering paladins.

The blood of man soaks this wood, he says, handing out fat maggot-like cigs.

Blood of man? says Key. You heard of Somnah City? A bloody fuckin battle, says Key. The streets are clay red, now, because of that struggle. Children watching from little hiding places as the elders of their families run circles fleeing from the encroaching onslaught of magicians and their soldiers, attempting to escape death with such a futility we believed the dead more fortunate than the living.

Doubt neither what I say about the magicians who came waving their hands up to Solus. I heard our troops exclaim, Good Gods, knives of ice falling from the sky!

Knives of ice...

Mind you, the objective of our attack was to root these magicians, you know, and the alchemy they turned against defenseless citizens. We survived their storms of icicle-like knives using shields and speed, and pressed forward through the city. Man, woman, child.

Seen a young boy crying beside an old man, who was dying, when an icicle shattered the boy's skull.

Knights of the Dark Horse Company used chains to strangle soldiers of the rebellion.

If a man claims the Knights of Mirshan are noble do not listen to him. Instead remind him of this day.

Our survivors we pressed on, into the city. The magicians weakened. Aerth grew restless. We mercs could feel that. And it had them afraid. Fear is the single most potent tool in war, and can swing a sword harder than any human or weaken one so as not to lift a feather.

Sure the magicians were strong, but we pressed on. Deeper into the city, we culled thousands of sympathizers to the magicians' cause and killed just as many in the streets. Those wizards worried none over their people, their supporters, but protected themselves only. That is why we destroyed as many of the crooked bastards as we could.

Then the Dark Horse Company, led then by Margon Sannacherib of Ataraxia, I believe, encircled our battalion. I didn't understand. We were on the same side. We were mercenaries, not apart of the Mirshan army, but we fought on the same side. Our squad broke off and fought through the lines and retreated. It was a hasty escape. Some of our soldiers were left behind, left to die. My brother was among those the knights had captured.

Zaer Rozkhe, a knight of the Dark Horse Company loyal to the Emperor, charged my brother with high war crimes including pillage, rape, and treason, which means, the key to my brother's cell is probably lost, swallowed and shit out the ass of some pig rolling round the muck of Ataraxia. And without me, he will rot until the knights see fit to execute him.

Watched my brother, then. They hooded him with a pillow case and fettered his wrists and ankles and threw him in a wagon. I watched them from a distance. It was a long walk out to the Djad, and it's been a long ride ever since."

"The knights of Mirshan left you for dead and you left your brother no better. Now, you're looking for him?" Jim says. "Your brother?"

Key nods. "Indeed. At the least, I should be there at his execution."

*

We can be nothing but quiet while me mind breaks open. A hot roach falls from me fingers and ary one looks at me laughing. Smiles are wicked-wick...ed. Ruttish rotten tears run a river on me cheek and I laugh, too.

"What's happening?" I cry laugh cry.

They howl like jackals except this wolf himself and the haunt beside me. She is a sad cat. Her lashes are whipping out, out at me. Look at me.

I go to stand but the bell tower booms above me or does it and I'm really dizzy and I fall dizzy to the earthen floor and the heavens turn me inside out and makes me again and still I spin with the walls closer to me than ever but dark like the space between the stars. I cannot find. I cannot touch. I sift through me lungs with me claws and crawl and climb to stand and I wander out.

Cold black watery sky.

Stars stripe the sky in yellow arcs like lightning frame and peels away layers of the dark Djad sands with the pearl fruit beneath me. I look up, look: glitter is star warmth in the heart. Wrayth follows me. Her sleepy eyes are loving eyes, intimate like, and she watches me curious as a lover.

The ridge is red and cold. It's leagues up to the top. The bell peals boom and bang and I dance why not. Let us go.

She says okay I will follow you. Take care of you, dear man. A long fall for anyone, can't you tell sweet man? Ruttish rotten lungs beat ceaselessly as we climb. I've a hot face and cold wet sunburned arms. Love her now because she's awake because any mind I've lost she has safe for me when I ascend from hell again.

Rocks in me hands are the knuckles of Mirshan. I feel em clink below me as we clamber climb to a small cliff. She has me close saying you're okay dear man. Wrayth's touch is star warmth and glitter and it makes the sky blank and pearl like the Djad floor so that all space I see is a shade of gray except her.

Higher.

No, higher.

We're there. High as we can be in the Djad and the closest to the stars I ever been. The church is below us a couple a yards. Lo, oh whoa– heavens.

Spit me out. Please. I'm begging you God.

Hollow earth under these boots. I'm dizzy. A long fall for anyone, she says. I toss out me arms, reach out wide and look up way up into the eyes of the universe and she bends me to you Wrayth.

That's smoke.

Yes it is. Rising in great tumbles, I hear it growl through the throat of a dragon and the smoke twirls deep into the night and dries and heats the wet cold black sky. There is a different heat in me chest.

I'll kill him.

You will not. Sit with me, she says. Sit with me. There is nothing you can do to extinguish that fire. Nothing anyone can do now. Let it die.

For now I nod and agree with her. Between that and wooziness, that's all I got. Wrayth tucks a cloak about me neck and pulls me tight.

It's a sad thing, she says. But sleep easy. The best you can.

I'm jostled awake by distant bellows, haunting death throes, cold windhowl. Wrayth is at the end of the cliff, her moonlit clothes and hair whipping and drifting away from her body while she stands unwavering. Two staves of smoke fill the predawn sky with mindless misanthropy. A bitter wind catches me lips and they quiver a bit.

"I'm sorry, Brap," I whisper, sitting up straight.

Wrayth turns to me very slowly. Dust moves across the ridge in heavy clots. She covers her eyes but I know they're watching me. Mindless, she says.

I nod. Still a couple a paces away, I feel weightless and sit back down. There is whiskey still swimming in me skull. "How long's I out?"

Not long, she says. Not long enough.

"No." I groan, laying down entirely. "But thanks for keeping me–"

Warm. You're welcome. These words are terse like a knife wound.

But as if she feels me pain, she steps and lowers herself beside me.

After she says, I think you should go back to sleep a while.

I smile and nuzzle my head into her gray cloak, but I don't find sleep.

At dawn, Solus wakes and we smell burnt paper. Sweat and blood replaces morning dew. Any and all cold dissipates. Wrayth and I are silhouettes atop the red cliff and no one will find us, at least not yet. The mercs are still drugged on fancy-ass cigs, wine, whiskey.

I can only imagine.

Colorless quilts swirl along the horizon and I know it now that Brap's soul floats in that wind and smoke, restless in the sky or dead arywhere but within me. Perhaps the fabric of his being hangs no more in that vast ceiling but instead drifts into the deeper parts of me lungs and sails along the river of me veins and into me heart and bides in me whiskey jug skull. And here it sits. Here it broods.

Sal must have killed him. Maybe all of em.

We should check it out, I say.

Is that a good idea?

I reckon not. When I sigh, it hurts. The pain is not subtle but it is not sharp, either. There is a slow grating in me throat.

Don't, Wrayth says. Oh…dear man.

I rest me head in me hands, and begin to sob. I cry.

Wrayth looks on. You're okay, dear man. She stands up beside me and walks to the edge of the cliff. You have to promise me something, dear man.

Do I?

It's no small and silly promise, therefore you must make it.

She looks away.

The wind kicks up her gray cloak.

It flaps noisily in the airy nothingness of the cliff's edge.

Beneath her are the leagues we overcame in our climb.

Promise me you will not become like the man who is not a man, with whom you travel. Promise me when I return here I will find you human.

I reason I'll never be like em, Wrayth. But I can't promise ye nothing.

Wrayth reads me in a way I can't describe. I could stare at her till time stops.

She smiles.

I look up at her, incredulous. Any concern towards her feels unwarranted yet strong. Can ye stay another night?

Not the way I want. She shakes her head. But you can't, either.

I look down.

The cosmos have entwined our paths one time before. Why not again?

Wrayth reveals a strapped knife at the side of her pale hip, fingers its sharp edge. She opens her eyes wide and watches buzzards circle fresh death while other birds of prey stare from high eyries, a trailing gaze down on the shadows of birds nefarious and flitting on the Djad's creamy-ochre blanket. Time to wake. That dear God, Solus, whose breath boils the moisture from the sands. Awake, all of you, he says. Wake.

This knife, dear man, she says. This knife was my dignity. I have it not for skinning game or carving wood. I have it to annihilate. I have it five years now...

Your father is an old man. Will ye kill him?

No.

God-sake. Then I will.

No.

I reason he needs stopped.

He will be, she whispers.

I look at her strange.

Then I will return to Mirshan. For you and this land.

Wrayth beckons me close.

I'm hesitant. And so she reaches around me neck and pulls me close. I don't resist. Take this, she says in me ear. I don't need the knife anymore. I feel the knife's pommel in me palm. The whole thing's heavier than I'd imagined a blade could be.

Wrayth holds me against her chest for a long moment and I feel her chin quivering throughout me whole body. I'm sorry to her. For the shortcomings of humanity, we are all to blame.

O, Hollow is this building of God.

Men and women here sweat and sleep on the floor. All except The Minister. His eyes slither in the recesses of the abode and he whispers to himself, something I ain't ever seen. Wrayth and I wake up the rest of em when we gather our trappings but we are careful not disturb the tense beatitude between us. The rest of em rouse and Blacksmith Jim drags himself to the cooking fire and fries food for all us drifters. Hen eggs and pig strip again. I force it down. Something about it all makes me uncomfortable, sick. Breakfast is silent. Jim's body of slackjawed cohorts play humdrum cards over they food while Key picks away any dull deposits on his khopesh. Shiv doses again bright and early. Slow but sure, his eyes turn blank.

The three of em go out back to retrieve they horses.

"Jim," I say. "Thank ye for the food and shelter."

His cold beady eyes focus. "Indeed. Travel safe."

"Sal comes round here," I say, "Ye be careful with him."

"I intend to," says Jim. "Well you get on out of here, okay. No need to have you here when I'm selling you to him."

A frozen lump hits me throat.

"Shit, kid. Don't act surprised. You have to kill me to keep me quiet."

"I ought kill ye, then." I'm conscious of the knife at me side, trembling like a bell staff. "Ye are meant for better ends, though."

Blacksmith Jim looks disgusted. "Hope he gets you, too. Bunch of dogs is all you are."

I nod to him, staring hard. "Well. Then this is goodbye."

I grab me pack and hoist it up. Wrayth stands before me, not hiding. The sun shines through the walls of this dark hall, shines upon us with graceful fingers, gentle warmth.

We have much to say yet, I think.

More than anything I fear solitude.

She blinks slow.

Mere hours ago I felt like we...don't leave me here alone.

*

Tempestuous drift—-

We ride toward a gaping black hole in the sky.

The violent pupil of a higher being.

The proficiency of God in the steep hatred of a storm.

It wells in carnation sunrise

the blue mountains stolen across the horizon

the ugly decay of gangrene

all prisms of the cosmos

mourning for the living

empathy

existence

Is it to know this work or to work it only.

Not so much a question as an answer.

O God help us.

Dirt and dust curl in gray funnels behind the hooves of our horses and climb like a tornado whirling up from the ground.

Thunder echoes a bass in the earth and wind swims through stalks of dead heath and bone dry sinopia.

Our horses ride strong, fast.

I'd been set back off my task, some would say.

The Minister eyes me. "Your map dictates Crawing isn't far. Are you true, young pup?"

"Indeed." I nod. "But a storm's brewing ahead of us. Maybe best to find cover again tonight?"

"Nah," says Shiv, barely with it. "Storm will do us good. And if nothing else, we put some desert between Sal and our pack."

I nod again. "We've much land to cover ourselves."

Shiv spits. "You reckon to cover it alone, pup?"

No, I say. "It was a weak warning I know. Crawing ain't so far. A hard ride through the night ought do us. If the horses can handle."

"They can," The Minister says.

I look at him strange.

They all laugh but me. He pets Redfur and smiles to the sun. "To Crawing, then."

"To Crawing."

I think of Wrayth when we're on the move again. Small visions of her sleep inside me memory, like a small candle never really burning but always warm. Yet pangs of conscience, cold in the sharpness of her knife bite the hand in which the knife rests.

It's slow going all day with the sun's hot lashes and humid blanket on our backs. Solus whips me skin shades of sunburn to something like a skinned ham.

Eventually we stop to heal underneath a single withering willow tree and watch as the storm taunts us from afar.

The smell of rain is mute on the stagnant sticky draft and it's pleasant. All day it's slow going.

Dry corn and salted meats and oat paste by sundown.

We look up and watch the dome fall crimson like the inside of an eyelid.

We drink in small sips the warm sweat and saliva of the Djad desert. Fill our canteens with the sugari juice and collect any stone arrow heads strewn about the sand.

We pray for rain.

The strain on the horses seems undeniable but they eat and drink less than any of us. The Minister hand-feeds Redfur a brown-spotted pear right before we're off again. It ain't much and it's almost rotted but the horse doesn't mind any.

When our bearings are straight as we like, it's time to move on again.

The Djad aureate and melting just before night.

The wind blows and twirls dust in its fingers. Key rides over ash black desert and the wind blows obsidian element and twirls dust in its fingers. There's an awful cry silenced by the thickness of the wet night air. It's over between heart beats: Key is on his back, looking to the sky. His horse is suddenly a skeleton; its flesh dryly tears from the bone and floats in the wind.

He wails about as though blind. "What in God," he yells.

The Minister rides by and keeps his distance from the black stain of dissipated horse flesh.

Key throws himself up and kicks the skeletal effigy into pieces. The dust settles around him and he and The Minister make long eye contact.

"Let me ride," says Key.

The Minister shakes his head. "Ride with Shiv. Risk only what is disposable anyway," he grins at me but I look away fast. "That is an Elemental Consumption Field, a result of the war; there must be an imbalance from the strength of the magicks used, then. Not even the nastiest of the nasty, young pup. Took his horse before you could blink."

I stare ahead, unsure what just happened. A bit of me closes again, keeps em out of me head.

Wrayth again.

The Minister suspects I'm not all here. He eyes me, careful. Watches the way I eat.

"You've become delicate," he says. "The meat is stuck to the bone. You must eat always on the run for no hunter can catch you this way."

I spit out a thread of rice and give him a quick eye. "I only run when something's chasing."

Shiv laughs loud. "Look at the boy. Hangs around the she-wolf back there, and now look at him. Got himself some backbone." Key bites his fingernails and spits em to the side. His narrow eyes betray his amusement.

The Minister replies with a coldsnap glare. He shakes his head and says nothing. Then he looks to the violet sky. He wheezes, a wicked laughter. "A storm is coming," he says, smiling. "How close is Crawing?"

"Close enough at this rate. Post-luncheon if we keep at it. But it's open desert. No daytime cover."

He nods. "Certainly possible with these horses."

"Ye need tell me about those horses."

"In time, perhaps."

"Be there another way?" I ask, gripping Wrayth's slender knife.

He shakes his head.

A horse dies beneath me and so sunup is bleak and grey. Lightning strikes silent miles ahead. Crawing is hours away. For hours then, I hang on Redfur behind The Minister. His scent is that of an undertaker– stakes and earthworms and rot. Never smelled it before. Haven't been so close, either. The wind stills and the Djad becomes greasy warm like cheesecloth. Soon something fills the air, seems to mummify it. The food in me stomach jumps to me throat– I all but spew, it's so foul. Vibration stolen on the waves, a buzz loudlike. Has to be a swarm growing closer. We move slow now. On the edge of me vision, it's like buried ridges.

The Minister hums as we move past it. "A dragon?" He laughs.

Shiv nods. "Used to be."

I climb off the horse, careful not to hurt me knee. "A what?" I whisper.

I limp closer, shivering. The spine is buried beneath the sand, a storm having blown past perhaps months ago. I follow the tip into the earth and out the end where its skull is without flesh. The teeth measure the length of me legs easy. That sends another shock up me spine.

Crawing is close. Outlines of sandstone abodes form like blots of pus through a bandage. Inhale and sigh, smile: we will soon be done. They will have no need of me, and I no need of em either.

Crawing is a great, but not large, town. Men and women peddle goods at the center, finagling prices at throttling volumes and guarding they caravans from the cutpurses who bob and weave about in crowds with yellow dogeyes and wet tongues. Give ye what? We hear people say.

Pilgrims too pass through here. They spread the word of they own gods while running with foreign coin. But that's a dangerous undertaking. Both because prakas terrorize the outlands and because people ain't keen to taking copper they can't spend at home. Mercenaries ain't uncommon, either. Like merchants, they have goods to sell but they ain't fruits, meats, or wagon wheels. For a price, many of em'll make ashes of a village. A little more, and they'll tear down Sargafa. Or try to.

We drifters come in to Crawing with our chessacks tight and our heads upturned. Encircling town the shape of a pear is saguaro fencing. Manmade towers flank the entrance; a pair of ripeskinned archers lounge with they bows set against the ledge. One whistles and the other spits. Below stand two more guards, well-equipped.

A woman, stout in a pale leather jerkin, greets us solemn-like. "Aye, Mousai, young *compan*. A good group ye draggin in?"

I shake me head but then laugh dry.

"Ah, it ain't good days to be foolin, boy. Word's gotten round bout you."

"Ought to keep it quiet that I'm here," I tell her.

She nods and wipes her upper lip. "Aye, ye ain't too late either. So keep yer trouble knotted up and ye'll be safe. Empire's ain't ever been too quick since I's alive."

I grin, tell her okay, and she lets us through. The streetfolk pay us little mind except in tossing us religious tracts or shouting for us to join the trade. I wave to those I know by face and name but Key grabs me wrist and all but breaks it.

"It was your idea to shut up, so do it," he says. I don't argue.

"Live-bait Tavern," I say. "Drop our horses out back and get ye all an ale. I got business elsewise."

"Sure," The Minister says, steering Redfur through a narrow alley.

"Key and Shiv will find the pack some feeding ground. Work, as you'd have it. Must have something, yes?"

I nod.

Children play back here, rolling bones and hopping boxes fingered into the dirt. Full of gaiety despite they impoverishment. Have em they innocence. All our movements forward separate those children from they playground and it pisses em off, but they scatter into the places of the town where the sun ain't to touch and let us on our merry. Others ain't always been so lucky. In bars I heard of em getting together with willow whips and broken billyclubs and cornering good folk with the threat of violent ends for the cause of copper. No one can stand against the swarm. I reason if Redfur hadn't her nose upfront, we may have been in for a tussle ourselves. But untouched we find the stable behind Live-bait and lead the mares in and keep em tied nice. Priea's on me mind again. Hadn't been so long since I'd be leading her here instead. I shake the thought and strut off without a word.

Around the other side, I stand against the cool rock and observe the fluid crowd and listen to it breathe. There ain't many white folk in Crawing. Too far from attraction. They ain't no glitz here like they got in Ri'shurai. Only intrigue here is who stole Sir Vegan's bull and butchered it up and fed it to him and his vegan family calling it new pepper. How hateful. How absurd. Whole town acts like circus folk, methinks. The world around em is blithely unfocused and those few aware reckon not to change it. Let the dull sands of the Djad be dull– we can be fascinating, they cry. Why do they mock the northerners? Liberty of Primalozza means freedom to rape others of the fruits of their mercantile labor. A silver for a wheel of cheese. Tenpence copper for some Dream-tear whiskey. Black as night, it is. Black as night, ye will see. A good slogan, aye, but I never remember any good ale needing peddled. Shit sells itself like those poor skinny women of the brothels. But women ain't sold once. While ye oft enough spew the whiskey, ye ain't to lick it back up. So they call em whores, then. May as well sell em for what they give out direct, on they own will. Men make women nothing but stock, a hen laying eggs or a female cow giving milk. Prostitution ain't the fowl name, but the stock name hiding spirits bound in ritualistic rape. I don't care if ye got a million copper coins. This is me godforsaken body. It's the gold-obsessed cock-driven world, Wrayth might say. If it were a gold-obsessed cunny-driven world, would I be a sex slave? Tough to imagine, but more than likely true. And inside Live-bait, The Minister orders a lady himself. May she pull his sack to his ankle, bloody and white. Key and Shiv get a round for a table and start chatting it up. Got any work around here? Shiv asks. Key looks demonic and remains silent. The perfect weapon. We got everything ye need right here, says Shiv.

I look around, hobble, scale the scene of Crawing's town square where the loudmouths and agitators cull. No mayor exists, only a council of five men and five women whose opinions all differ. On days they ain't to meet, a clerical type sits in and handles daily civ business. Here ye are, put ye mark there. Now ye owe ten pennies when before ye owed twenty. It's a mess but most governments are. Burrowcratic. Anticipating another meteor storm. Into the meeting hall, I'm looking for Rozkhe's agent Chaw. He's in a back lodge wolfing down a late lunch. Some assortment of bread, broth, and drink.

"A bit early for that." I smile and nod to the pint.

He looks up midbite. "Nay, goodsir. Never a minute too early for some glumfin black," his mutual smile dissipates. "Ye got me that letter, aye? Ye better. Rozkhe could all but make it here before ye. Lucky duck," he says. "He'll return to Quriah no longer than four days from now. He expects to see ye."

"For what? I ain't been there on work," I tell him.

"Well," he dips a chunk of bread and sops it in his broth, shoves it down with little swallowing. "Ye gonna vishit now," he says. "Another letter we got for ye. Important. Clashified."

"That's brilliant. I'm all but bound for home and I ain't even got a horse."

He swallows and wipes his mouth. "Eh," he says through a veil of contemplation. He seems to be considering something suspicious, a plan, before uttering:"That's a hell of a band ye traveling with." He lowers his head and slurps from a clay mug. "Hell of a band indeed."

"What do ye know of em?"

"Eh well, not much. Rozkhe has a hit for a man looks much like this guy." He jabs at a poorly drawn warrant labeled: Three Orphans of War. Loosely I can imagine one of em being The Minister, darkly as they got his face. Nothing captures the sight of his snake eyes but the withering of a soul. "Ye ride in with em?" he asks.

"Could be. But it ain't nothing. They got me here, saved me life from the dirty hands of... I'm grateful to em, aye."

He nods and reads something below the caption:

The Minister.

Whorehouses are not pastimes, but lifestyles.

Grain ale, lantern light, dose.

He is given to hell.

In dealing. In suffering.

"Sound like yer men?"

I swallow and fall flush. There's a reward on his neck. "Get me out of here then," I say. "Sal al-Matugal has fire on me tail. A hunter, Chaw. All me life I been out of Mirshan's view. I help a few men who saved me life and I'm an outlaw. A tenday's passed, maybe less. I need away from em."

Chaw's eyes soften. He pulls a silver piece from his coat and tosses it to me. "Put that in yer boot, fella. Call it a gift from Crawing. Now," he says. "Mirshan needs ye, Mousai. Even if they out to kill ye. Sal's on renegade status with the Dak-thaz Company. So ride out his pursuit, get to Quriah. This message needs to sit in Rozkhe's hand not too long from now. He pay ye well, boy." He rolls a tight, heavy scroll to me. "A list of prisoners being stationed who need hanged. Rogue mercs, bunch a treasonous bastards. This is an article born of..." he says and takes a stiff swig of glumfin black. "Sargafa, Tahtne, Saris. Leaders with personal vendettas. Who's who of hangings. They gotta consider who'd make good slaves too. Can't be too strong or intelligent or they'll rebel. Too weak and they ain't worth a night with a toothless whore."

I shake me head and grit me teeth. "Still ain't got a horse, Chaw."

"Means nothing," a voice says from behind us. "Found us a job."

Chaw's jaw opens a slight. Whiskey spittle dots the corner of his mouth. His eyes are white with fear.

"That quick?" I mutter without turning back to him.

"That quick," says Shiv. "It's a little off path. But we're all going that way and The Minister wants ye to come along, pup."

"Is that so."

Shiv chuckles and leaves quiet as he came. I think to meself, By God how much did he hear?

"He's a tough lookin bastard himself, Mousai. Good, I say. Use em for some protection. Get a ride out of em while ye at it."

"Are ye goddamned crazy?" I say.

He shakes his head. "Hell if they taken a likin to ye, what ye got to worry on?"

"Thanks for the silver, Chaw. I've got to move on, get out of here. A shame ye couldn't help me," I say and pace for a few seconds while he stares into his soup bowl. "Call em bastards but look at ye. One sight of em and ye shake in your skin with the notion to face em. Fine. Hope me body turns up," I say. "Heartless is what ye are. A blackguard."

"Ah spit on ye, Mousai. Get on outta here."

Out of view, I grip Wrayth's knife until the blood is cut from me fingers.

No. Simply no.

I leave, limp out to the white hot noon where me shadow's gone to hide and the yellow stained traders rest under cloth shade that hangs from Crawing's grander abodes, speaking of far off lands over limegreen tea and thin cool ale. The sunscorched sky vibrates, fallen to punish the sand, wavering all vision. Dizzy I sit in the shade of a pale alley. Live-bait has put up a pavilion of sorts. Silks hang over redwood benches which are tightly occupied by these pilgrims among travelers among foreigners among humans among animals. Sheep bleat they throats out and horses snicker in lone sarcasm. Redfur has more conscience than her master, methinks. Humans naturally do form the feeling of guilt. In our blood it broods, pumps through our heart through ary vein.

It is evil to me, then, when one person can deal another pain without feeling pain they ownselves.

Wind gusts through open windows smelling like fat fleshy worms. Meanwhile, we are lounging, lined around a thigh-high table playing a dice game I ain't played before. It's The Minister, Shiv, three local ruffians, and me. Where Key got to, who knows but him. Anyway these men they got blackjack clubs sitting on the table beside they copper coins to keep us off em and they women (if not they wives) are near enough to keep a spying eye on us too. All of em are oliveskinned folk like me, wearing loosefit shirts and gritty cravats about they necks and it seems none of em care to keep clean shaved. Blue flashes light up the Live-bait Tavern and then escape us, leaving the hall dim again. I take a drain from some smoke and cough it out and take a drain from me ale and take deep swallows and exhale satisfied.

"It a git to hailin soon," a man spits. "From a sounds of it."

The Minister grins at me from across the table. He coyly flicks a copper off his small stack and it rolls into the pot.

I shake me head. "Need it." I utter. "The water."

One man in particular gives me a second eye. Chubby man whose sausagelike fingers tic around his wooden mug. When he drinks from it, glug glug glug, ale foams around his lips and dribbles down his chin. "I ain't in this one," he says.

I drop too and his lazy drunk eyes stay on me as the move passes to Shiv. Around the table it goes, click-click the dice, and The Minister rakes in a pot. Oh, and the groaning they give. I chuckle at em behind me fist and lean back. Live-bait tavern swims on waves like a little rowboat and I throw fire down me throat with some whiskey and chase it with cool ale. I drop out of the next round and watch chubby.

"What are ye called?" I say to him. Shiv rolls a dosage and lights it, all eyes on him. "Chubs," I say and he looks me way. "What are ye called?"

"Eh," he belches. "Name's Ful-qu. As in. Fuck off, kid."

I grin. "Right, then," I say. "Ful-qu Chubs it be," I give a gentle laugh.

"Little prick... To hell with ye!" he roars and slams his fist on the table. In his fist is extra bone, extra dice. "My turn yet, yeh mutts?" he says with a huff, heavily amused. I quit me giggling and give his fist a dark eye. Glaring, I am.

Shiv blows a ring of mindbending smoke into the tavern hall and twitches by himself and lets his dice roll onto the floor. "Yee," he says and they're roaring again. All of em shake in obnoxious laughter that certainly erupts straight from they beerfilled bellies. Each and ary except The Minister, who amidst the chaos looks like Law itself, the black pupil of a higher being. The deadened life of a tempest, or perhaps, the force of the storm wrapped up in flesh. His snake eyes are careful over our new friends. I grin and lean up to the table. Chubs's dice are laying closer to me than to him and Shiv's are settled near the pot. I pull em toward me and palm one of the bones.

"I'm in this'n," I slur and it brings the gang back to the table, none too stolid. I roll em and get a decent set. Keep three and roll the others. I rake it in and drain me ale. "More," I cry.

By this time Chubs and his folk are losing all they coin to The Minister and me. Avarice and suspicion replace any good cheer the ale and the whiskey had to offer us and ary groan from they winnings gets us a second look, then a third look. Our little game gets quiet. I'm a little slower but I start to get how the game works. I watch Chubs and his men and sometimes they replace a bone with one in they palm and I can't tell if they're hiding it or not. All of em doing it but The Minister. He's playing it a bit different and still winning okay. Action to me and I call it quits for the round.

"Gone cheap now boys," he says. "Ain't ye gone give us a chance to git our coin, kid?"

"I reason not to," I say and smile thin. "Ye had the chance to win mine all this time, ain't ye?"

"Aye," he admits.

One of his get a small pot. His slackjawed ruffian friends hoop and holler, praise God.

Roll me bones out and it ain't spelt out too well but neither is Chubs' hand. I furtively glance to a barmaid and switch a bone with one in me hand, put it to something favorable. When me fingers inch toward me coin stack, Chubs slams his meat-paws heavy on me wrist.

Growling he says, "That how ye winnin, kid? Ye little cheat?"

The table is quiet.

I swallow. "Doing what ye did, goodsir."

"Callin me a cheat now?" he throws himself to his feet, still gripping me wrist. He rears his right fist into the air and I'm too drunk to flinch. I hear a clunk and the table rocks unsteady. Like a vampire, The Minister hovers over it and coming down the other side he puts his claws into Chubs' throat and shoves him into a wall and, like thunder between clouds, the tavern trembles. Chubs' eyes are wet and pink and his puffed up cheeks are turning the many colors of Mirshan. The Minister guides him along the wall not blinking not moving those eyes from this man's soul, and between em there is no light. They disappear with a flash of lightning. We listen.

I know the sound.

A fist, many fists, landing like hailstones. Broken nose, I hear. Over and over, the fists and cries and squeals like that of a dying rat, a dying man behind the shade of our diffusion— we can't stop him so why try— pleading for a "stop" because he has kids because his wife don't work because he will miss em wherever he goes if it ain't to em, "stop,"he cries. Stop. But more we hear while the crying slows to a rhythmic chirp. The Minister is only using one fist now. One fist in the defense of a young pup in the pack. I hear him quit. No voice to this man's soul now. The Minister walks from the backroom and no one speaks. Blood is dripping from his elbows, hands, from his patchy beard. It sticks to his eyelashes and those teeth he bares in combat like a jackal and he licks his grimy teeth clean and clenches his fist solemn and still, not a quiver in either hand, nor in his snake cold eyes.

"For you," he says to me and then looks to the rest. Shiv goes, ha ha and drools and The Minister ignores him.

"Was this. . ." I start. A couple of men whisper near the bar, grab for they weapons.

"It was, young pup. Do nothing unnecessary. The world in which you live revolves at a speed that offers no mercy and offer it in return you shall not. Another move from your friends," The Minister says to a ruffian. "And their throats, the each of them, will be split over this tavern and town and their blood sanctified by the natural order of the Djad. No one, not even you will remember him," The Minister says.

The crowd in Live-bait wanes with the promise of no return.

"Sit," The Minister says and the men sit. "Finish this game," he says.

Wrayth's knife is in me hand when I limp outside and watch the lightning shatter the sky. Black clouds drift in shards over the Djad and cry out angrily. The thunder in its voice rumbles the earth and soaks it with soupwarm rain. Crawing's nightwatch is bobbing around town with spears tapping against people's doors asking how ary one is. They armor looks sleek in the heavy rain and more so when the sky rips into pretty white pieces. Wind howls and barks and brings clots of mud up and swirls it like a bola over the town and throws it into buildings and ye can see it gathering power, rising up off the earth like a corpse coming to life. It dies only to reappear elsewhere. Me hair gets good and wet and I comb it away from me face and now rain's the only thing worth a smile.

The Minister did what he did for me, he said. Saved me from death, did he? A bad bruising, aye. I peer back to

Live-bait and lowly lit by lanterns the game of bones continues. Sitting on The Minister's lap is a barmaid and she's petting his scratchy cheek and sucking on his ear. Wrayth's knife grows cold in me fingers and I look away.

*

Crawing empties as the storm seems to calm. Streets are red and muddy like heavy clots of blood and a few denizens of Crawing slog through, more limp and hunkered than zombies back to they graves. The red mud cakes up to they calves and it all makes me sneer. Stubbornness keeps em out here, nothing else. If Lunus were out, so would they be. Call it arrogance, too. Mind me a dance, dear? they utter, the drunken buffoons. Fire in me chest squeals hypocrisy, so I laugh.

Redfur incites a riot at the over yonder stable just before God brings it down on us again and I lean back beneath an overhang and smile at its power. His voice is the wind, low and cold and roaring. The men of Crawing hustle into the dark caves of they abodes and look out through the sliver between a shutter and the wall and they weep about the anger of hell and they cry out "we love the land" and "ruin not our crop this year." He answers with hailstone and lancing blue streaks in the sky and quakes that seem to emit from the desert below and not the storm above. The nightwatch is out and one of em spots me and slogs through the street of blood with his dark cloak ahead to shield himself of the mud and he moves to me slow and careful, his spear slung.

He is obsidian in the face with white eyes that glow even in the tempest night. "Get inside ye," he calls. "To the Live-bait, aye?"

I shake me head.

He halts. "Was less a question than ye actin, kid."

"I am not going back there."

"Trouble afoot?"

I look away from him and spit. "Something like that, I reason."

"Well."

"I ain't in any trouble. If ye want just forget about it. Ye ought to anyhow. For ye own sake," I say.

He comes closer and I don't move any which way. Under the overhang the rain stops pelting him and he's breathing heavy, his glowing eyes sullen now. "Now," says the man. "What ye sayin, kid? Ye done wrong?"

"No," I say. "But me ears have."

"More, kid. I take easy on ye if ye get honest with me right quick."

"It's me company," I confess. "Two of em in there, one's dosed into shit and the other, The Minister, he's. . ."

"Aye, son. Show me," he says.

"No," I stammer loud. "No, they'll get me. They'll get me, he's too– " and that's when I notice Key at the corner of the alley across the way, making sharp that curved blade. I fall silent.

"We'll get a group after em." They ain't, the nightwatch ain't listening.

"Look," I say and grab him up by the straps of his armor, push him into the wall. "Let em go or ye will die. Ye ain't seen what they do, ye ain't seen it."

Unalarmed, he shoves me into the mud and kicks me over to me side and then again to me belly and he rolls me to me shoulders and stands over me, pulls me chest, neck, and head limplike close to his face. "Now I told ye, kid. Wanted to take it easy on ye."

"I'm honest sir," I cry.

"He's honest," says a ghastly voice. Key plunges his blade down behind the man's skull and the bloody khopesh uncorks blood from the nightwatch's throat and all over me it sprays and continues to spray while I scramble and claw away like a cat in water. "Don't move, Mousai," Key says. "Don't."

I lay there on me back, a constant sheen of warm rain cleanses me face while I look at him horrified, panting and looking around for witnesses but there ain't none. I don't move, can't. The body of a dying man shivers in the cold making noises of suffocation and he clutches the dirt and his eyes like candles dim as his soul departs from his flesh and still I fail to move. "Ye killed him," I weep. "Like ary one. Fuck," I say.

"Aye," Key says and wipes the man off his blade. "Three times now we saved you."

I cry out and grab me ribs. "Rather ye fuckin kill me."

"Would if The Minister ain't taken to you."

"And what the fuck are ye afraid of?"

Key laughs and leans down to me. "Less than you'd like," he says. "To your feet. Come on."

He ropes me up by the hand and I feel like a leaf helpless in a river.

Key leads me through a back alley and we end up behind Live-bait anyway. He says, "Shiv tells me you have something that'll interest me."

I squint, uncertain.

He stabs the wall behind me violently and then fixes his two cold narrowed eyes in a glare. "A list."

Coughing I look around and shake me head.

"No?" he says quietly.

I shake me head again and he smacks it with an open hand. "Listen to me. My brother's on the list, ain't he?"

"Not a damn clue," I say.

"I need to see the list, the names. Now, god damn it."

I reply, "Take em," and give a breathy laugh and dig into me pockets and find nothing he wants to see. Trouble is I didn't look at the names meself. "Soon as I can get to it, it's yours."

"That a pup," he says.

I smile weak and thin. "Ye are all fuckin monsters, hear?"

"Aye," says Key. "And you're no different. I imagine it will take time, but you'll see it too."

"The fuck are ye talking about?"

"Shut up," he says, shoving me along. "And get me that letter."

Key thrusts me into the tavern where Shiv's sitting by himself, his eyes rolled back to his brain. He gets worse ary time I see him. The game must have ended not long ago because coins still lay on the table and a pair of dice still has some quiver left, though that may be from the storm. It thunders again and its rumble echoes the throbbing in me head. Key weaves through a small maze of overturned chairs and collects the winnings on the table without a change of expression about him and looks around assessing it all.

"He has a woman," I say.

Key nods, doesn't look at me, but kicks me chessack out from beneath the table. He moves to Shiv and clutches his face and gets real close. "Might be dead," he says and his head shakes slow.

"We need to leave here. Two are dead because of ye and that blood'll draw Sal right quick," I say, checking behind the bar for buckets, find two empty ones and a hooded pail of rich whiskey and gather em both up.

Key grins but doesn't say anything.

He wants the list, fine. I give it to him. He unfurls it with both hands. His slitted eyes drop just so and I see his face contort only a slight. His brother's on the list. I know it.

The scrolls winds itself up and Key tosses it to me. "We will need you," he says.

"What for?"

"We'll fuckin need you. Just shut up."

"Ye breaking him out? Your brother? I can't be involved with—"

"You are involved. First, Mousai, we ride for the Cavity. You know of it?"

"Aye," I say, confused. Why there? It's full of bandits, war veterans. God damn, why there?

"We have friends there," he utters. I can't tell if I should believe him. "Mercenary days. It's a small band, maybe twenty. Sal knows of the cavity, knows of its inhabitants, knows he can't take em with a small band. The Cavity'll give us some shade."

I turn away and me eyes well with tears. None of it feels right at all, but it seems they got me caged. Sal would catch me if I took off because these towns know me.

Cold dread fills me bones when I think of going out on me own, against prakas and Mirshan both. And cold dread takes the color out of me when I face Key and he makes a satisfied expression that says he knows exactly what I'm thinking.

One thing to be trapped, another to be tortured.

"I need ye too," I whisper.

He nods and takes up his khopesh. "I'll get The Minister. You fetch the horses."

"What about Shiv?"

"He'll live." Key disappears into the room where Chubs was killed. I hear him raiding the corpse and can imagine his narrow stoic eyes ravening over another man's kill with quick hands, cold fingers.

I tighten me chessack and step outside. Two steps into an alleyway, I lean against a wall. The tears come but the sound of em is lost in the torrential cascade of rain. I ache with hatred. Home, then. I think of home. The simplicity of love there, the simplicity in all of it. We had not motives but inspiration. We live for each other's lives.

And blood. What blood? Blood is our Aerth-force of life and blood is spilt so often that it colors the desert quicker than Solus himself, who is or for Godsake must be gnashing his teeth over the Djad, over those of us who fill it up, and empty it likewise. Oh imagine it: the barren hot waste with empty cold men scuttling across. Men who assert they own-selves through violence but who ain't man enough to see the stupidity.

Revenge? The most violent selfish act. A pleasure of fallen men who have no self of they own, no breath to speak of, no heart and no passion. This is the worst of weakness: Key will reunite with his brother, and that is the least of it. I know Quriah and Zaer Rozkhe. The pack knows what I know.

They'll get him, and it makes me worse.

I can't stop em.

A young pup caged, snared by wolves. I can't stop em without becoming em.

The knife is in me fist again and me face grows cold and these hands they go cold and I take up the knife and me eyes open wide and the fog in em clears away. A light wind passes through me hair and cries in the hollow of the alley, lulls me so that I stop and drop to me knee. I can't do it. I can't.

I can't stop em.

Under cover of shade we depart by the northern road. Crawing fades into heavy mist and I watch it go with the cold feeling that Sal's real close behind and the storm won't wash away those footprints of ours left in innocent blood. He'll find us. I think of Law-qen. I think of Brap, Fancy. I think of the evil curls of smoke that filled the sky; they are still in me, suffocating me in sleep suffocating me when light hits these pupils and still I can see how it could...

...But from here– strapped onto Redfur with The Minister slogging through the Djad for the small city of Quriah– the world is sad and cold and unmoving despite our slow trudge over it; despite knowing there is heat in the stars behind the clouds above, I see only the ruin...

The blood in The Minister's dreadlocked hair and the blank look in Shiv's eyes and the emotionless wall that is Key's face. Square ridgelines form over the horizon where Solus hints at dawn, cerise like a slice to the bone.

"What is this place?" The Minister whispers. "There is smoke coming up."

"It ain't unlikely," I say defeated. "Call these ridges the Fossils. People of way back thought they were surfacing skeletons of a race of titans or something silly like it, and ye can see all around the scars of they shovels. Tried to dig em up. Never did, though."

"How silly is it, really?" The Minister turns his head a slight back to me.

"Think about it."

Key looks to us and then looks away.

"Think of it this way: If you were to starve by some failure in the hunt, young pup, the very fact you did indeed hunt extinguishes your failure."

"The fuck ye talking about now?"

"Or think of this way," he goes on. "What emptiness lays waste to the wolf that waits beside a rock for the pack to bring it food? The way of the world is action, Mousai, could you disagree? More so, it is movement. Movement, young pup. So as the wolf starves without having hunted for its food, people starve not having searched for meaning in their lives."

I sigh silent, and look away from the fossils.

Throughout the day the storm swirls like indigo dye stirring in some god's pail. It stays ominous but distant and quiet, to either side of us drifters. Odd as hell, really: storms in the Djad usually hit hard and then break apart before anyone has time to shut they gaping mouths. Besides that, we of all people deserve its punishment. By the look of it, we ain't yet safe from it either.

We ride slow. The humid land where small fields of raw vegetation lay flattened beneath the pelt of fist sized hail. Old houses abandoned and empty. Those fenced arenas where chattel had grazed at one point in time strewn the only life I've seen in what feels like months: dead gilded fields, beautiful in a naive way. Too small to be great, too great to be small– I watch it closely as we ride past. Wind walks through it and moves the bronze in gentle waves as though invisible little children play in its midst. The Djad surrounding is cheerless. And a day away, Quriah. If ye look hard, its bellied towers gleam golden on the horizon. But by night we will have reached the Cavity, a reputed den of brutal outlaws.

Redfur neighs and gods be damned it sounds of laughter.

*

The Fossils are teethlike indeed: square, well-spaced, and gritty. Skinny mountain goats hide in any umbra that the labyrinthine crevices create while Solus shines over gnarly arbol, old knotted trees casting slender fingers of darkness over the fossiljaw walls. Little spiders and scorpions wrestle for cool sand beneath the surface, leaping out of hiding only to trap they prey like hungry cutpurses stalking the flats of strange and foreign Sargafa.

But here, the Fossils.

Old teeth of old Titans preserved to confuse us. It says to me how young I am. As we approach I think of a lantern going out, putting to dark what I may think or may have thought about this place.

Nearby, The Minister sharply snaps a limb from a tree and gives it to me quiet and calm.

"What's this for?"

"Walk on it. It's for your knee. It will be a trek through the tunnels– up and down, slick turns. No use hurting that knee, took long enough to heal so much as it has."

I nod. "Ye ever been in a place like this?"

He shakes his head but says, "Yes." The Minister looks haggard, sleepless. "There is a camp here already," he says. "Best to make use of it, though the company met tonight may be less hospitable than can be hoped for."

"I reason not. They ain't the kind to just take anyone in, I know that one thing."

"They'll allow it, young pup. And be charitable, you watch. Wolves are kind to their own."

"Are they?"

He sucks his teeth. "They should be." For a minute The Minister strokes his dusty beard and scratches at his nose, idle and still.

"Well, come on," says he, and we go.

The tunnels of the cave are shaped like knotted rope, lit in certain areas by mucus colored lichen that leaches driblets of water from the Fossil walls. Some places are thin and we're barely able to stand and some parts widen out twist turn dip and rise without too much notice. We trudge slow and the horses are more than pissed off by the lowlight, but they seem to move over the slick cavernlike floor better than we do. When I look hard, I can see that Redfur's hooves are sinking in like it's mud– but it's not mud, to be sure. I give The Minister the eye; he knows what I see, but he doesn't answer the questions on me face.

It seems we're scraping along for hours, wandering through a maze of low-lit tunnels and dead ends. I tap the little walking stick as we go, a bit bored I guess. Sweat runs down me chin and we move toward the huzzbuzz of flies on death. They swarm is close because little stragglers are in me hair and brow, me skin.

"Ye know where we're going?" I ask scratching frantic as fuck.

Shiv, behind me, laughs.

"Shut up," I say, not in the mood for him. "Anyone know?"

"Outlaws extract the fungus off the caverns. They leave only the path which leads to their camp," explains The Minister.

"What?" I twist in a circle as if to ask Shiv and Key. They don't know either. "Shit grows itself?"

"Slowly. But yes," he says. "Gathered perhaps by the younger men or women who are not skilled at hunting."

"Aye," I agree, spitting out dust and little insects. Annoying shit, I tell ye.

"What do you know?" Shiv says and his awful little chuckling echoes throughout the caverns. "I ain't seen you hunt since I know you."

"Ain't known me long, either."

"So you hunt?" he says in earnest.

The Minister raises an eyebrow.

"No. I don't. Family's a farming family."

"Right," Shiv says. "You don't have the kill in you," he says and I note this as his first ever compliment to me.

Key smiles and looks forward.

Then Shiv says, "Wait...that Sargafan. A straight shot pup." He shoots an invisible arrow with an imaginary bow.

Redness fills me face while he laughs a bit more. I shoo away clouds of gnats and bugs, think about stabbing him between the ribs.

The Minister wipes the air with a dismissive hand and Shiv ceases his giggling.

Shiv says, as if the thought had crackled over his lips, "We have much—doe much dosage left."

"Don't do it now, jackass," Key says. "You'll make us all loopy."

"Nothing wrong with that," he whispers, licking his lips. "Well how long do I got?"

"Not long," The Minister says. "The lichen is fewer. Pickers are out here over-picking. Must be closer to the camp for it to be familiar ground."

Familiar to whom I do not know. But I'm not excited about meeting em, whoever they might be.

*

We are quiet when light reaches its white hand into the narrow opening. The Minister leads with his hand on the cavern wall as it grows tight– getting Redfur out will be no small thing. Peeking out, his snake eyes look up and his face is golden in the sunlight while his body remains hidden with the rest of us.

Four spears stick into the ground from above, dropping a prison swift, but not swift enough to really catch The Minister. Two dusky men land on they feet and circle around, hungrier than lions.

"Any of ye with province? With Mirshan?" and me intestines grind and knot, knowing I'm technically employed by a knight, who is sanctioned by the Emperor.

The Minister snarls and kicks through the barrier of spears in one heavy gust. "No." The Minister beckons us with his ax. "Come, pack," he whispers, and we climb out. The look on these men's faces is blank. Not afraid, not happy. Blank.

"Ain't here for Mirshan," Shiv grins.

"In spite of it?" the one sentry asks.

Key nods and goes for a walk. No one stops him.

The Minister says, "Listen. None of you are in danger. Not from any hunter-killers. These you see are the remnants of a mercenary company. Fought at Somnah City, and lived. Mirshan wants to keep it quiet, but now you know who is here. Each of them is an efficient hunter."

"The kid?"

"Indeed."

"You?"

The Minister smiles.

"Hafta speak with Lisburn, man."

"Present him."

"He'll come out to ye," the guard says. Both, I notice, are well-built, but not large. They muscles are diamonds, tight gems sculpted from stone; sweat sticks to they black skin and gnats stick to they tan clothes.

The Minister nods and his eyes wander. Mine wander with.

Within the cavity are hundreds of manmade shelves, all constructed from looted wood and twisted arbol and willow vines. Linen the color of dust stretches above natural tunnels and alcoves that more than likely lead to personal apartments or privies– which may be one in the same. Above us is a rope ladder leading to a rockform jutting out like a balcony where these two black men usually wait with they spears. Upon the wall nails suspend limited weapon racks, each equipped with a bow and quiver and four javelins each. Ahead of us, though, a trail leads into the mountain where a curl of smoke signals exactly where the rest of these outlaws spend they time—around the food, that is.

One of the guards struts to the entrance of a small alcove and yells down it for a little backup since he doesn't trust us any.

I wouldn't either.

Behind me Redfur neighs and stamps her hoof.

"How the hell ye get out?" I whisper.

192 / THE PAINTED LADY

The Minister ignores me, but Shiv releases a little giggle. What a prick.

"Aye," the man says. "Keep a watch on em," he says. He goes, "Get a bigger guard if ye need, yea. But I got to get gone."

"Where're ye gone to, boyo?" another asks from behind the dirty linen. Sounds grouchy.

"Oh well we got visitors, did ye know?"

"Ah right, yea," he says and steps from behind the curtain wielding in his right hand a bottle of whiskey and his left hand a maggot of a dose.

"Oh," Shiv smiles. "We shall, I say. How do I say? We shall get along fine."

The man is a white man tanned. And husky. Got a lumberjack's frame and a big head. He sucks on the fancy cig and grins to us. "Yea. No need for another guard," he jests.

If only he knew.

Shiv snorts but The Minister strikes a venomous look that silences any jokes, even those not yet spoken.

"It is dangerous out there," says The Minister. "For anyone. But particularly for enemies of Mirshan."

"That what ye are? Outlaws?" The man huffs and pulls at his belt, pulls his britches up a notch.

Shiv chuckles. "Yes, that's about it."

"Fine, then. Fine by me."

*

Those two share a shot or so of whiskey while I examine Redfur from head to tail, all the time petting her.

Not long after Key comes back from whatever he was doing, probably pissing, and he is followed closely by four dirty looking men led by the obsidian skinned Lisburn himself. I don't imagine older men leading, but here he is: He wears a stark white goatee, nappy like any Sargafan's. But his eyes, how interesting. They are the both of em blue. He walks as though on sheep horn with the caution of a prowling cat. He motions to Shiv's new best friend with a silent gaze.

"Mercenaries." Our guard addresses us as though he hadn't our attention before. When our eyes refocus upon him he says, "I'm Raulk. Call me yer new Cap if ye want. If ye live here, it means ye work here, means ye work for me. Only reason ye work for me is because I'm the only fucker out here who knows what work needs to be done. If ye know too, feel free to fuckin tell me. Lisburn does. Now we don't like to kill round here. Don't know why. Guess too many bodies brings too many hunters out here and then we gotta deal with them, most likely by killing. That becomes a mess quick as the killing. We don't avoid killing either. I should be fair and honest with ye. Not a god damned Sargafan here who isn't a god damned praka when he needs to be."

The Minister grins and puts his ax and blade away.

"I got more to say," Raulk spits. "Since all ye are green, we'll want some kind of payment or at least proof ye can take care of yerselfs for a few days till yer work contributes to the group and our resources will be surely sufficient."

"As discussed," says The Minister. "This pack is efficient at hunting if there is in fact game."

Raulk stomps with one foot and guffaws. "Yea," he says. "There's game now. The oasis starts a couple hours out. Ye spend yer whole fuckin day out there and you can come back with one hell of a meal for yerselfs. But wildlife isn't keen on getting killed. We gotta chase them in circles round the oasis. All the while protectin the young and females. Eh. Come back for them later, though," he says.

Satisfied for some reason, Lisburn shows us around. The complex is centered by a ramp of sorts that curls up to another level of the Cavity. Jagged spires encircle the encampment, forming natural watchtowers that offer a great deal of cover. And it seems they have dug a tunnel from the bottom up– one level to the next– whose belly is like a furnace, all smothered in black ash. I imagine they use this to heat the earth above during those icy nights of the Djad.

The upper level is packed with small tents, around twenty. One larger stands pretty tall and wide, probably the home of old Lisburn, but I don't know. Women walk up, having followed us along the spiral ramp, toting clay buckets of water.

"There's a water source?" The Minister sounds pleased.

Raulk nods. "Cavity used to be a military base, man. They irrigate from way out, on Lisburn's design, couple hours I told ye. Now we got servants workin there. Make fuckin sure they keep it goin. Good thing about them is they ain't in no way afraid of Mirshan because they used to be servants of a couple of goodins in the Dark Horse. They know the goings-on. Had one of our scribes record it."

Leading to a bare patch of level stone, Raulk stops and pets his chin. "Looks like a good place for ye to sleep, yea or nay?"

There is a burnt-out campfire surrounded by heavy stone and covered with a grill and spit, all newer looking. Certainly loot from stolen from pilgrims passing along the river to the east. In the near distance I hear hammers hitting stone with some constancy and I spin around and see no men, not anywhere but the four or so with us.

"Thy look," Lisburn says suddenly intense. "A confused grimace. Look not worried young, young lad. Those men thou seek hath gone to their duties. However, tonight!" he says. "Thou shall meet them, and they shall meet thee. A fair eve for faire, I believe."

Raulk grins. "Indeed it is, old man."

I swallow, not having heard such a speech in me life, not outside of me dad's tales. "I ain't worried," I stutter and it hits me how stupid I sound.

"No, let us imagine thou hath no thing about which to worry."

The Minister eyes him careful and I can see his jaws tighten. "Not anymore than you, he doesn't," he says through a thin maw.

Lisburn puckers his lips, near laughter.

"Don't know about you, but I'll sleep anywhere," Shiv interrupts. "Get us a tent, we should be fine."

Aptly distracted: "Make the damn thing yerselfs," Raulk groans. "Enough stolen lumber out here to build a forest. Aye." He laughs and looks to the quiet Lisburn. "And we have."

Having found new curiosity, The Minister says, "Must see this forest."

*

"That's a beautiful thing," The Minister admits.

I am quite frankly surprised to see a small forest when they show it to me. Sure it ain't much, not at all.

The irrigation pools beneath a semi-circle of greenery and makes the soil fertile. Fruit dangles from the thin palm trees and desert pines and little saguaro plants surround the sixteen foot trees like a prisonyard fence. Two men have rope ladders tied to thicker branches and have buckets in they hands filling those buckets with coconut, sugari, and waterapples. Mules stand at the base of a fruitless gray line of trees. Redfur and her companion horse go to it natural, happy under cold shade; they anticipate being tied.

Quiet, I tiptoe the stalks of the trees and peer high into they branches while The Minister and all em speak of other things. One man eyes me from his perch and calls. "Watch yourself," he says and slams a smaller coconut to the ground; it breaks into brown and white little shards, gray milk splatter near me feet.

I smile crookedly.

"Don't stand there stupid. Pick through there and eat it."

With careful hands I piece me way through the meat and gnaw on it happy and it's delicious.

Raulk steps beside me where I kneel and says, "Yea. It's a good fuckin fruit right?"

I nod and smile dumb, drooling the milk. "Never so fresh."

"Aye well. Yer friends are off to hunt, then. We hadn't kidded ye about it. But Lisburn has something for ye. Mind walkin with him?"

"Not at all," I say. About willing to do anything to keep away from me own company. "What'd ye have me do now?"

"Ye don't mind walkin with him?"

"No."

"Nay? Well find out from him then, son. Don't keep him waitin either. He hates that shit."

*

Lisburn waits for me by the horses. He's feeding em kind and gentle. They take to him quick. His eyes, when they look to me, shine like blue steel. "Ah," he says. "Hath the day gone under the horizon already?"

"Not yet."

"I want for thee a friend. He's but a boy to thee. No matter," he says and leads me through downward slope into another system of tunnels. It seems to be a narrow hall of sorts, like ye'd find at an inn, lit by rusty oil lanterns that hiss as we walk by em. Hacking and coughing cries emit from curtained-off alcoves to either side. Crotchety old women and men, sick women and men. It's upsetting to hear.

Lisburn doesn't address it.

Rather, we plunge into darkness where wilted possum haw hangs above the alcove entrance on our left side. The small room is yet dank despite the dry dust that blankets the mudcolored dome; splinters and shavings and lifelike statues all of clay or stone clutter the infirmary which houses a boy younger than me— he may be twelve. Pale bone is his skin. By the light of a dying candle he works.

"Call him Sculptor," Lisburn whispers. "He bears his name self-evidently. An orphan much like the rest. He is sick. Nothing contagious, it seems, or lest we'd all have it. None of us understand." The old man sighs. "However, soon he shall die. I can feel it." He turns to me with fierce eyes afire. Not anger, but fervor. "Perhaps ye could walk with him today. Forage or hunt for food if it pleases thee. Sculptor knows the routes."

I look at the boy. He holds a knife in his hand and works it over pieces of stone with strikes so precise I'm sad to be reminded of Key and his dreaded khopesh. I shudder at the thought: If that were to be this kid's future I may be inclined to slip me hand over his mouth and show him something of death, so scared I'd be for him to see anything else. Are there those who think such things of me? Had Brap? Had Wrayth?

Where will ye be, love, when I need ye?

Mousai. I am here with you, dear man.

I hope that is true.

I am here.

Don't leave from me.

*

I kneel beside Sculptor, a child. "Ye like being called that? Sculptor?"

He pauses in his work. "It's not bad." His voice is joyful, and innocent.

"I suppose not. What are ye working on here?"

He chuckles for a moment. "Well, it's."

"It's?"

"You tell me, goodsir." He slides his piece beneath me view right quick. At first I'm astonished. What appears like little logs stacked into cabins and, more intricately, into a near-perfect model of Quriah as seen from the easternmost ridges.

I lose me breath a moment, am forced to give him another look. He's proud of his work. That much I can tell. I grow immediate admiration. "Ye been here, to this town?" Pieces, some no bigger than toothpicks, fit together beautifully. And all of it whittled by those little white hands. I laugh quiet and turn me head back. Lisburn smiles before he disappears.

*

"Skinny bunrabbits play around here sometimes," the little boy says. His bright eyes are big wanderers, eager explorers. I can tell by looking at em he knows the Cavity well and has done all the exploration his eyes have allowed him to imagine. We move quickly about the complex, in and out of shadow and sun and blood colored halls and citrus-scented alcoves, but all the food we find is the graygreen fungus sticking slimily to the walls. Sculptor takes his carving knife, handy at all times I guess, and scrapes a bit of it into his bucket. He notices me not moving.

"It's all we're getting, goodsir."

I frown.

And he frowns back.

So I at the very least help him fill the bucket full of this greasy fatlike fungus, even though he knows I ain't too happy with it. It's messy and the shit can break open if ye don't scrape it just right and when it breaks open, snotty mud drops out of it like gray egg yolk. All over me by the time we get a bucketful– and that gives our young whittling sick-thing a chuckle or two.

Fine then.

"How long have ye done that?"

"Done what?" He looks up at me as we begin our windy travel back to the encampment.

"Those carvings. The statues and arything."

"Oh," he says. "Them always been real easy. I like doing the work. Started when I was even younger." Sculptor extends his arm as though to pet an invisible dog. "Bout that tall," he says. "Well, first one I ever did was one of them Fire Eaters. I chiseled several limestone slabs and then I..."

Where had I heard that name?

A force in the military. Legends, all of em. Said a hundred men in a company went the whole War without a casualty. True or not, I ain't likely to ever know. I remember dad telling me how they got the name, which was a lot like any of the names these soldiers get— the more obvious or ironic, the better. During a fight they'd perform the tricks of charlatans and illusionists, spitting fire into the eyes of they enemies, scorching hair from the flesh and flesh from the bone. Where they went they left ashes of enemies. Had I even heard the name Lisburn before? It ain't likely.

"How'd they turn out?"

"Not well." He giggles. "Coulda been lots worse too. Maybe I show you then."

I nod and look straightforward, limping alongside Sculptor as he navigates the warren of tunnels beneath the Cavity. He's a quiet kid unless talked to. Reminds me a lot of children in me hometown.

He ain't afraid of these men who ain't like him in ways he don't understand quite yet.

Eventually we get back to the sickhall where new wooden crates, about a dozen of em, are stacked all the way down through the corridor. Silks and Swords, they read.

Another hit of banditry.

We move past the crates, which tighten the hall up so that we both have to sidestep through, and slip into his curtained-off room and find it no longer reserved for Sculptor.

Sargafans are huddled up beside the kid's bed and to the floor, they faces bruised in a pasty melon-like texture: eyes swollen shut; lips split like fat worms; noses broken smashed flat. All the boy's sculptures are in crumbled up pieces, on the floor.

A black iron chain drags over miniature Quriah like an infernal anaconda.

Sculptor doesn't notice.

He looks to me eyes filled with water and then he looks to the injured men.

"Come on," I say and grab around his shoulders to lead him away.

He wiggles out of me grip and shakes his little head. "Let me," he says serious so I let him go. He sets the bucket down and goes back into the room and piles the scrap pieces of wood in his arms and walks em back out and says, "Grab the food, goodsir," so friendly I want to sob.

Later
Later I see him with his chisel.
Carving new lives from stone and clay –
Even lying lowly
in the thorn bush with grisly beaten dogs
(carnivora of all kinds)
I see, through the shrub,
the white haven of Solus.
I hear, through the violent throes of hounds,
pipes humming low in distant humility.

*

The sun wanes behind the jagged horizon, the sky a metallic ocean where birds swim and plunge into it like flying daggers dipping into mercury. Birds and bloodsuckers without identity in a void without name. Lizards lazily stretch out now, out of the shadows cool in the day waiting for the shadows frozen at night. Solus waves goodbye. His fingers flicker and I feel the warmth of God removed without remorse (without whim), regular as decay is to a reaper.

*

Let the faire begin—-

The sword dancers come and dance and glorious is the whirl and wham of those once wan weapons coming alive they clash just barely sounding like rain on a tin roof sparks fly as though fireflies extinguished to the regal gardens grown in some paradise that now grows here before our eyes like spirits dancing from our bodies watch the wailing whirl and they clothes wrap around and confuse and swirl in they silks leaping like arcing sparks em-selves then they spit fire as they are famous for and bladed fans open and fade and send smoke into the magic of the nightfall like a stream of moonbeam the swords gleam and the dancers bow (bravado!) and become the birds before a storm and disappear disappear disappear disappear disappear disappear.

*

Then the albino leopard, a she-leopard albino, paces her cage. Men wheel it near the fire where her meal chars to a black-skin oblivion and whiskey makes the Fire Eaters laugh. They tease it. Sometimes with stones. She is sad cat. Thin and tired, smelling of piss and fish.

Later into the night I sneak a heavy lump of mountain rabbit, hog marrow and fresh fungus– a lump of food that had been me own dinner– between the bars of her cage when she ain't paying attention– or when she pretends to pay no attention. I want to pet her ear and briefly I reach in to do so. But I keep back. Afraid of what may happen.

*

Come come circle round! Hear ye, Lisburn's Song!
There is no war but the war within,

No battle for good; no battle can
Protect the good from
The violence of the battle.

—- Look at his legs when he dances, I whisper. He's like a halfgoat.

*

Tonight in the decayed hollow rock, The Cavity, singers sing and flutists pipe. Can ye hear the strings hum at the fingers of the fiddlers? The bows glide sexy. And lo, beautiful harpists: the drunken plucking. They eyes are sunken and closed. But look at they hands, they long hair wet with oil and grain ale.

One of em catches me staring and

I don't apologize, but I do look away.

Later I stumble through the carnival trying to find Sculptor but where is he? Ain't nowhere to be found.

Other lads are and they look pitifully alone and confused like…well…lost children, I suppose. So I push me chest out, ye know, real far, and I cry: "Children! Ye be in luck, fer I…tell stories, and ye'll want to hear this one."

There I become a candle by they bed at night—a whisper of a flame, consuming wick and melting wax.

Among the children is the harpist, and she's elated, methinks, to be awake.

"And ye too?" I say to her.

She smiles lazily and raises her tankard. "Onward! Tale it like it is."

*

Now listen to this.

There was once a young sorceress by the name of Synthe Ceresa, born thousands upon thousands of years ago.

She was beautiful by the standards of any thinking thing whatsoever.

But unbeknownst to her, she gained the attention of a cruel and unkind baron, so that one day, in a fit of extreme madness, he captured and dragged her into a hut and there, hidden from the rest of the villagers, the cruel and unkind baron drugged her fast asleep. The drugs made her dumb, made her speech impossible, so that the baron was free to come and go as he pleased, without worry she might scream or cry for help. And from then on she was always sleepy.

Until one morning, when she was in a drowsy stupor and the baron was collecting firewood, a serpent slithered into her hut through two twigs in the wall of the hut. Unaware the serpent was her fey, the magical beings that serve all the greatest sorceresses, she became really scared and what would you do if a snake crept upon you, except scream? But her scream was more of a sssssss. And the serpent coiled and leaped up, then snapped the side of her neck. Snake bites are usually venomous and this one was no different from the usual: The venom placed her into a deep comatose sleep.

Now, when the big ugly baron returned to his hut, his arms full of lumber, he discovered what he believed was her dead body, she was so fast asleep.

Fearful of being caught, the cruel and unkind baron decided quickly and coldly to lug her corpse to the wide river, now called the River of Sleep, and that's where he dumped her body. She was so light, and the vein of the river so deep, she floated, just beneath the surface, and when she sank, the serpent swam beneath her back to keep her from truly dying.

The River of Sleep took her all the way south and out to sea, where a current ripped her to a sea cavern.

She rests there now, in a deep magical sleep, waiting for the birth of prince charming, a man she might speak to in his dreams, guiding him to her place of rest and sleep, to reawaken her from her magical slumber.

*

Ragged shawl hanging loose from that harpist's shoulders. She ain't wearing much else. Look at her hands. They ain't soft, ain't rough neither. Restless hands of the harpist. "How much've ye drunk?"

"Give em to me," she says in me ear. I feel her busy hand reach the rope around me waist. Our hands meet.

"How much've ye drunk?"

She shifts her hair to show me her neck. Presses into me. "I haven't much, lad."

Her hand drops from me britches and she stumbles back. Grabbing her by the waist, I hoist her up in me arms and I hobble toward an empty cot. She's telling me how she wants to fuck and I'm telling her how silly she sounds. I lay her across the cot and wrap a dirty cloak about her bare legs and she's kinda smiling at me in a sexy way.

I lean down and kiss her forehead, whisper: "I love another" and the harpist shrugs her shoulders and, still smiling, closes her eyes.

People shuffle about the fire like undead. I've never seen so many drunk people in all me life. No one's paying attention to us, so I sit against a rock beside her cot and rub me hands in the dirt. I sigh.

She says to me: "I know. Because. I know you."

Her drunk talk makes me laugh and I lean back and watch the drunkards all of em in they dance, how sweet it is in some way. How sweet life can be.

Feel the midnight air.

The wind picks up, grows cold under me arms. I hear a whisper, "I know…" But the harpist is rolled over and I write the name of me love in the dirt and the wind blows it away.

I wake bolt upright. Early to a red dawn and me brain's swimming in a jar of ale. Shiv and Key are fast asleep, snoring.

Shiv has two fingers on a blade, another two on dose. The Minister is nowhere in sight. Just like him, I suppose, but I get curious. Here around the Djad nights are icy but mornings I can bear with a heavy leather jerkin and some cloth sleeves. Daytime burns like whips.

I grab me walker and try to stand. Leg's bothering me pretty good but I got no use to complain and no one to complain to. Horse huffs at me. It sounds like a laugh so I grin and give her some oatmeal. She looks empty without her rider, The Minister. I suppose we all do.

The road to Quriah is not a long one, not from the Cavity.

Shiv tells me: "The plan, pup. Yer going to want in on it now. Back in Crawing, we was looking for work. A bounty. So happened that a large bounty's on Lisburn's head. The Minister tells him about it. Tells him also that, after Faire, after all the Fire Eaters have fallen asleep drunk, that we the orphans can easily fulfill it. Lisburn is of course not nervous. He's old and satisfied. But he don't want death either. The Minister informs him about the hunter-killer Sal, how he's been trailing us and we need him off. Ye want to strike a deal with mine company, he says. The Minister answers yes. Key already implanted the rumor that we'd be here and that we'd be here as long as it took to win their confidence– then we'd strike."

"He's expecting us to be there."

"Aye."

"But we ain't."

"Well," Shiv says. "The way we figure it is this: Sal won't storm the Cavity without a sizeable gang. He realizes that he's the enemy. He's coming into an empire in its own right. He is not the law there."

"And we have business in Quriah," interjects Key.

"Your brother."

He nods to say basically.

"We will free him the night of or night after our arrival. And return to the Cavity."

"I don't get it," I tell em. "What's this to do with me? Why would I return there?"

"Pup," Shiv laughs. "Where else can you go? If we don't do this, Sal will catch up with you and kill you and take yer pelt to the Guild in Crawing for his reward. But follow us and Sal's as good as dead."

"Lisburn agreed to set an ambush," says The Minister. "Said that under only the worst circumstances of luck could they find themselves a casualty," he snarls. "But not to worry, a deadlier pack will reside there; thus, even if the Fire Eaters fail to slay Sal, he will not soon return. You, young pup, will be secure as a pearl."

"Where were they this morning? Lisburn? All of em?" Thinking of how they'd all disappeared, god sake.

"Preparing," his answer is quiet.

I shake me head. "No. I can't do this. What, commit more crimes against the empire in one night than I had in the first place."

"Perhaps that much is true," The Minister says cool. "But they distinguish not your one crime of treason from the other. You are now an outlaw. Until you face their penalty— which is death keep in mind— you will remain an outlaw. When they find you, you will die." He looks deep into me, whispers: "You decide daily. Live or not to. Decide again."

I can't do this.

But I do it anyway. "Will we have to fight?" I whimper.

"All depends when we return, pup. If Sal shows up before, then no. If after, then yes."

"I ain't killing anymore."

"So be it," The Minister nods.

There is a lavender haze on the horizon.

Above it, she is sleepy, silken– Lunus a white cocoon.

I lowly stare at her as we stride.

Her light guides me the entire night.

Behold, Quriah—

It is called the gateway to Sargafa.

A small palace, whose onionshaped watchtowers overlook the city like dim candles, capping the northern portal in moonlit quiet. But I'll deceive ye not: its gates are heavy with traffic at all times. Pilgrims from Saris come. Vagabond merchants and traveling minstrels go. Hard-eyed mercenaries three hundred yards outside with they weapons strung to they hips whisper the price of they utility to the seedier types as they move along the bronze road. Mirshanni outriders circle the limits as the worst equipped warriors in the empire. They exist more for census than for security.

Long before we reach the south gate, a small band of these outriders hail us. We slow our horses for em.

"What business have ye?" he says in a typical officer tone.

"To see the executions." Key tugs the leather reins toward his chin.

"Oh?" the outrider sighs. "The courier ain't yet arrived."

"No," I announce and give Key a dirty look. "He's...I'm right here."

"Mousai then?"

"Aye."

"Rozkhe needs ye pretty quick."

"So I hear," I say. "It's me last letter anyway."

"What ye mumblin now?"

"It don't pay well enough what with prakas and wolves always on ye."

"Mind if I check your chessacks and baggage?" the outrider says.

I keep talking, knowing Shiv's got drugs on him: "And it don't even work right. Who do I convenience but a rare few?" I'd hate to sit in prison with Key's brother.

The pack is silent while the outrider glares at me. "Perhaps," he says. "But till we get a better way, get on."

"Ye know. I reason I'd like to."

He shrugs, sniffs the dry air and allows us passage. Shiv keeps his drugs and we keep our heads.

I keep the letter, may as well.

*

Bone weary.

The sun stretches the sky in one solid stripe.

Time

slows.

Here's Zurrey, following a family of foreigners, asking em for money. Key recognizes him.

"He must have escaped."

"How the fuck would he do that?" asks Shiv.

"A bribe? Maybe fought his way out I don't know, but that's him."

I can't recognize em as brothers.

Zurrey appears like a square-eye-socketed beggar with stringy muscles tight to the bones, no fat on him, on his face nothing except hair and thornbrush on his head, his eyes sunken eyes so dark they seem without sclera wilted rotten deep in his head, his chapped lips a perfect gray-pink line, now he's happy to see his brother, happy to be free, happy to roam the desert without chains on his knees and arms, or a hammer on his hands, the hot stones—

Key grabs Zurrey by the shoulder and leads him to the shade of an alleyway. "Tell me, then, whose cock you suck?"

They embrace. "That isn't funny. They almost broke me down," says Zurrey. "But I knew somehow to expect you. You wouldn't leave me for dead a second time. I knew it."

Key lacks sentimentality. They walk off alone down the busy thoroughfare while The Minister smokes in the wheel-grooved streets, amidst the trudging mules and horses smelling like the straw and shit they sleep on.

I follow Key and his brother into a tavern and sit at an empty table and rest me head in me arms while they drink harsh liquor and talk of things I can't hear or understand.

Soon they're drunk and soon we exit Quriah through the eastern gate, on foot this time, and it's like I can walk in that kinda heat without thinking any so it feels like within the blink of an eye we arrive at Zaer Rozkhe's estate—

The Minister orders me to stay put outside. "Guard him," he says to Key's brother, Zurrey. The shadows of crooked trees are long, and in em I cower.

Over Crawing, and the towns behind us, days away, the storm silently lights the sky in blue sparks.

Oh God.

Nervous. The man who owns this home gives me an honest living.

I pace around the front of the house, prop meself against its white-wooden walls.

"You ain't going in there," says Zurrey and repeats himself whispering.

The house creaks. Wind.

I pace in front of Zurrey again.

I consider him, he's skinny, not too tall.

I shove him. Don't even think about it. I leap off me strong leg and shove him to his back, and he scrapes through the dirt. I climb on his chest before he has a chance to sit up, and I ball up my hands and strike him I don't know how many times. He's dazed. His eyes blank. I collapse his nose.

What's come over me? Like a sickness.

I falter over the threshold of Rozkhe's house. The stone floor, the pale wooden walls.

It's dark inside the house, it feels haunted, like there are faces of souls in the boards of the walls and I hear em in the walls, suffering men, given to hell –given to The Minister.

I walk numb through a long, dark hallway.

"Leave them," a man weeps.

I can barely hear.

"Leave them," he says. "You have me, leave them. Oh please, must I beg you?"

I follow the vibration through the house.

Tiptoelike limping with me hand on the wall.

An instinctive shiver takes hold of me and I stop to listen, afraid to press further.

A woman's voice or a girl's voice a ripe voice a muffled voice.

God, oh God.

I limp through the house navigating its rooms, the moans the violent shaking the stop, stop, stop, stop, I get lost in nondescript rooms, stacks of tomes, and empty weapon racks, broken lanterns, suddenly soundless rooms.

One loud shriek sends me left, through of a studio room with smashed lutes and crumpled drums and splintered easels ripped up canvas and into a hall charging towards light.

Silhouettes fill the light.

A back door, opened, to the light of the Djad.

Rozkhe is naked, a broken creature.

His dislocated jaw flops around his collar bone.

His wide open eyes run with pink water.

His wife huddles, kneeling, her forehead smudged against the house.

Shiv stumbles away from her, weak laughter, and he stumbles with his cock unbound, white cum nasty stretching dripping on the floor.

He doses, laughs.

Stumbles, laughs.

At first I can't move.

Rozkhe's children weeping and kneeling beside they crying fearful mother and quiet old Key watches em and now his brother Zurrey hunched forward panting behind me, gripping the frame of the door.

Two boys, convulsing uncontrollably, kneeling —

oh God so young

Why must this have happened?

When The Minister looks at me, I fold in two, and fall with them.

"That little fucker hit me," Zurrey says and spits blood.

Key unveils the khopesh and stands cold approaching Rozkhe's wife and mother to they children.

Shiv hovers over the knight's back and tightens Rozkhe's black cravat around his neck, chokes him, forces slow dying— and Shiv slides real close to this knight of the Dark Horse Company and grits his teeth.

Key has blood on his waist and crotch, where he cleaned off his khopesh. "Pray, zaer," he says. "For your wife and children, pray." Key's smile is like the foul grin of a cadaver.

Wrayth's knife feels like a single spear from the sun.

Key raises the khopesh. He ain't looking at me.

The Minister's eyes flit and blink. He looks at me quick, says nothing, stands still, straight, saying nothing. He is frozen still; I can't explain how or why.

Numb I charge towards Key
Escaping Zurrey's grip
I'm numb
Shiv slams Rozkhe's face into the dirt.
Rozkhe drools blood, with Shiv atop him strangling him and the knight's children are in the hands of monsters.
I'm closer, I'm there
This knife this solar flare leading me
Key's khopesh slides beneath the mother's chin where she kneels beside her children, and tears
stream down,
like mist against desert heat.
I have to stop em,
somehow, no matter what happens after.
I drive Wrayth's knife deep between Key's ribs
and I pull out the knife
Red, hot, blood
Sticky
and again
I stab him
in the middle of his spine
again in his spine
the blood on the knife
and Key stands straight and the knife sticks there
in his spine
bowing like a tree limb
I yank out the knife and it drips blood
Key's khopesh drops beside the woman.
She exhales.
She mustn't believe it.
The children are quiet, except for snotty inhales.

And Zurrey explodes into motion again, lunges at me, snarling,

I'm not thinking

his fingers clawing at me eyes and nose. I fall backward, into The Minister and he yanks me to the ground.

A sliver of steel penetrates flesh: the sound before the silence.

Zurrey's eyes widen.

The Minister thrusts forward and shoves Zurrey off his knife.

Wine dark blood bloats from the man's stomach.

"It's done, Shiv," The Minister whispers.

"Fuck that," Shiv says. "And fuck you. We're not finished. We got bodies on us now. Why did you let that happen? All these witnesses," he says. "Ah motherfucker what? Drag em inside and what? Bury em in the cellar?"

The Minister looks at me silent and still, ignoring Shiv, and then crouches over Key's corpse, fingers to his neck and wrists, and then his brother's; they are both quiet like the law.

Shiv's yelling, "We got to burn the house. Something. Anything. Can't let them live. I know that. Are you listening?"

"Shut up," I say, "I'm getting these fucking children away. Hear me? I'm getting em gone. Ye ain't getting in me way. Neither of ye. Step aside."

"No way. No fucking way they can walk. Rat us the fuck out. Here what yer pup's sayin, Minister?"

Then there is chaos inside the house. The splintering crumbling of furniture, the walls of the house. Shiv's punching the wall or headbutting it and his guttural ancient curse yapping through his teeth. "Yer wrong about this one. Yer dead-fuckin wrong."

"Shut up! For the love of god shut up," I say.

I kneel to Rozkhe, whose dead-gaze eyes stare at his children: "Get your children. Tell em to run far, OK? Hear me? Go on! Ye and I might die today," I say. "But not these."

"I can't," he says, shaking his head. "I'm dying."

"But not these."

All at once there is an abysmal chorus: the wife, the children.

Shiv's shadow upon me.

He strikes me.

I fall unconscious.

*

Buzzards hover atop the roof of Rozkhe's house.

I look at em blurry-eyed and down at the red-hot sand and, feeling weary to the bone, look for The Minister, who's standing outside the front of the house with his hands pressed to his chin as though praying, tendrils of dark smoke spiraling from his nostrils and lips.

"Are they dead?"

He says nothing. His eyes dilate.

"Oh why'd ye knock me out if not to murder em? Are they dead? All of em, are they dead? Answer me, I swear to God."

"The knight only."

"Prove it. I need you to prove it."

The Minister shrugs. "You want to die with him? Walk in the house, with Shiv."

"You're wrong again. Again and again and again."

I want to annihilate all traces of The Minister from the Aerth so badly but I know I'm incapable, not face to face, not now, maybe not ever. I try to sprint to him, crying and falling in the dry little rocks, rising on me good leg, falling again, again falling. When I get near him, I claw at his shoulders, rip him within inches of me face, and he resists all reaction.

"God damn would it matter if I put you down right here. Are ye even human?"

He forces me away with one hand, stands up, turns away, to enter the house.

"I'll go around, Minister. I have to see. I have to know exactly what ye done."

His back is still turned to me as he walks into the house.

Like me body perishes to stone, I don't follow. I can't.

And then,

Within the blink of an eye

the entire house:

the tongues

and whips

and flares

I can't comprehend how or why, but someone incinerates Rozkhe's house, and...

And the children... I couldn't hear em or see em, ye understand now?

I don't know if they escaped.

I don't know if they escaped.

That's everything I remember.

I don't remember any more.

I told ye everything I know.

Everything I know and remember.

ABOUT THE AUTHOR:

Benjamin Allen thanks his family & friends. He lives in Reading, PA, where he walks dogs, recycles, and freelances scholarly articles.